CHAMP: THE MISANTHROPE OF

THE YEAR

By

Erik Pollet

D1521640

For My Wife Lisa,
My Muse,
My Inspiration,
My Encouragement,
Without You There Would Be No Champ,
I Love You

Part I: ANGELS WITH FILTHY FACES

Part II: MY HEART FLOATS ON THE BOTTOM OF THE BOTTLE

Part III: THE FAT MAN SLEEPS WITH THE SWEDISH FISHES

PART 1: ANGELS WITH FILTHY

FACES

1

Within the city that you won't find on a 'Best Places to Live' list exists the 'Double Down Saloon'. In an alley behind this bar, three very large gentlemen are giving a beating to someone in a fetal position.

The man in this unfortunate situation is Champ. A nickname which derives from his birth name. Which is something the self-proclaimed private detective refuses to share. This is the story of Champ who may possibly be a better punching bag than he is a man.

I do enjoy spending my early afternoon on the floor clutching my knees. All the while my esteemed drinking chaps continue to pummel me for something I can't remember doing. Oh right, I think I called the big one's mother a four letter word.

In this position it's hard to tell which one is which. They all seem big and dumb. Their feet and hands seem to find all the meaty parts of my body despite trying to protect myself. I can't help but reflect on how this is a direct result of my winning personality.

As I start to think a change is in order I then remember I'm content with myself. Maybe not at this moment, but usually. Pity is a thing you should not waste on me. I guess there's a few things that needs to be said about myself. I can't be bothered to remember everything at this moment.

The first and probably most important fact about me is I have **congenital analgesia**. It's a rare medical condition which prevents my body from feeling pain or temperature. This can come in handy in situations like this. Unfortunately, it made a thing like growing up difficult.

During the melee that took place on my body I heard a loud crash, I thought they finally broke something. When it triggered the halting of my compadre's activity I was confused. When I try to get up with the intention of dusting myself off and to pick up my teeth I realize my assailants had run off.

I walked over to the noise's point of origin. A car is parked by the curb at the end of the alley. Crushed on top of what used to be a flat roof, was a body. There lay who-the-hell-knows-who. It's just a mangled corpse covered in blood. Staring back at me.

I called the faceless men, those are cops. Don't like calling them. It's like having to get a needle in the eye for me. I realize that analogy falls short coming from me so I assume that's what the equivalent would be.

I stand in front of the car, face bloodied, a black eye, a fat lip, and other bruises starting to form. Just staring at the body. Sounds of sirens getting louder behind him. I contemplate.

The bloody body lying a few feet away from me is a young Hispanic male in his early twenties. With his eyes still open he has a blank expression on his face, it's kind of creepy. It might mean he was calm as he fell the 12 stories. Or he could have been on a huge high. So says the fresh heroin track mark on his right arm.

The faceless men and ambulance sirens stop in front of the crushed car as I stand on other side. They brought along a special guest to the party: a TV news van.

Tonight a WCNT news exclusive!

A young man falls to his death from a 12 story warehouse roof hitting a car. Our very own Alison Soren is on the scene... Alison?

"Thank you Kurt... I am downtown at the grisly scene of what some sources describe as a suicide. We have an eyewitness with us now. Sir, can you tell us what you saw?"

"Yeah, I was getting the crap beaten out of me until I heard that poor kid's body smash down on the top of the car. I don't think it was a suicide by the way."

"What makes you say that sir?"

"How the fuck should I know? Oh wait, I'm a Marlowe. Or a private detective. If you know this poor schmuck, my name's Champ. My office is downtown 745 Kirby street, that's 74-"

The second thing that needs to be known about me is I get thirsty very often. I long for the sensation of the cool smooth liquid know as alcohol to go down my gullet. After all the excitement I go back in the bar to spend the rest of my money. Those new chums I made before are gone so as long as I keep my mouth shut, I'll be OK.

Which might be difficult for me to do depending on the situation. Because piece of information number three, I have no filter. What this means is I get my ass handed to me quite often due to my mouth. I could try to change this if I wanted to, but then I'd have to care.

I sit at the bar with ice on my face wounds as I drink. This is just an emotion I go through. After spending my whole life with this 'affliction' I don't consider myself a victim. Especially most of what I get into is my fault.

The ice helps with the swelling. I still need to be able to see through both eyes. It's becoming harder to breathe. The hutch helps me ignore that problem. This is my motivation for the things I do that don't seem to matter. In the end, I'm just pretending to feel.

This self-analyzing isn't the issue at the moment. My mind races with reasons why that kid fell off that roof. This is the inquisitive part of my personality.

Which brings me to the fourth piece of information on the subject of me. Despite my apathy towards most things when I pose myself a question I must answer it. I analyze, question, and research until I find the solution to my equation or problem.

My curiosity and the need to solve is my OCD. It can be quite obnoxious but comes in handy in my 'day job'.

I sometimes pay the bills as a Marlowe, or a Private Detective which is also number five on the list. When I say 'sometimes' I mean whenever I feel like it. When I say 'bills' I mean what the hell are those? As for 'jobs' I once did one for candy. I searched for someone's keys. It was a lollipop, it was delicious.

That news crew didn't appreciate the fact that I used naughty language or how I plugged my booming business. So I was cut off short. Overheard the faceless men on the scene mention how this was just an overdose. Didn't seem like any more attention was going to be paid to this case. Makes me wonder.

This leads me to number six on our get to know your local drunk asshole. I tend to talk strangely. Mostly talking about my slang. So keep up. Take the word hutch for an example. That's my word for the almighty sweet nectar of alcohol.

It may be pretty similar to hootch, but that is just a pedestrian word for something so much more complicated.

OK, this is a bullshit explanation for why my word is better. Then how about it just is?

That's it, the inside scoop on yours truly. Anything else is a need to basis and you don't need to know. Ugh, this whole experience has become cliché and makes me feel dirty.

It's time to take my leave and head to my office to get some sleep before the blackouts come. I down the rest of my drink, say goodbye to no one, and walk out into the sun. You can imagine my surprise that all I walked out into was darkness.

My office is at 745 Kirby Street in the downtown neighborhood of Graveside. At one time this was an up and coming area with movie theaters and coffee shops.

Now what remains was once described by the current esteemed Mayor Loeb as 'worse than bombed out downtown Bagdad.' What's the opposite of gentrification? That's right, abandonment.

On the second floor of the dilapidated building is my office. 'Champ – Private Dic' is on the front door. I didn't have enough money for all three words. So the painter took his frustration out by expressing how he felt about me through his art.

Spray painted below in red is the word 'Deadbeat'. Another love note from a fan. As I open the door I almost trip over the small mountain of bills that lay on the floor. This is including the letters still stuck in the mail slot.

My right eye is closed shut. I've sobered up on the way here. Instead of heading to the blackouts, must sleep. Never even checked myself for anything that could be broken.

My couch smells less like a garbage dump compared to most of my office. This spot will do well as a makeshift bed. I don't normally go to sleep without one foot in the blackouts. I have to take my chances. Until tomorrow and then doing more of what I truly do best, drink.

2

My sleep is interrupted as I am awoken by a knocking at my door. Along with crying from the other side. I can tell it's not tomorrow. Although I was groggy as I opened my good and less of a burden yet dry and itchy eye. I must not have been sleeping for too long.

I eventually open my door to find a young Hispanic girl standing in the doorway crying uncontrollably. Her perfume, which reminds me of cinnamon starts to fill the air within my office.

Mascara is running down the sides of her face that needs to be wiped off. She seems embarrassed, but not enough to compose herself. Certainly not enough to cover the cleavage that's pouring out from the top of her low cut top.

As I continue to observe her up and down I notice a tattoo on her right shoulder. It's covered by the right sleeve of her short sleeve top. It gets slightly uncovered every time she pushes her hair out of her sobbing face. It happens often. It's the fact that the tattoo looks light. As if it's covered in makeup. Maybe it's laser treatment.

It's these reasons that makes me notice. It was a triangle with the bottom line missing and inside is the letter 'A'.

This is what I do. My curiosity and questioning are one of the crosses I have to bear, as well as my pessimism.

You may see a scared, sad little girl. I may not. I don't trust anyone, I question everything. I stand and stare at what's going on in front of me. Frozen like a deer in headlights waiting until I figure things out. Much like I did at that kid's body. I like to call it zoning.

Maybe I'm being cold, but I haven't seen much that shock's me at first sight.

After what seems like a few minutes, I ask her if I could help her.

"I need your help Señor." Speaking in an I-don't-speak-English kind of accent. "Mi Hermano, Mi Hermano, he died."

Figuring out what she's saying from my very limited Spanish I ask, "Who was your brother?"

"You know him, you find him on car, I see you on televisiŏn." She said in-between the crying and sobbing.

She begins to explain to me that she doesn't think her brother died by falling off the roof while O.D.-ing. He was known for doing Heroin, but that he ran drugs for some drug kingpin. She thinks he might have had something to do with the brother's death. Since the brother probably stole for his habit.

I tried to explain to her that I don't care, but as nice as I could. "I don't care." She didn't seem to understand that. "Look, don't get me wrong, I am a little intrigued by this. There's no incentive though. Where would I start? I'm so busy as it is-" Yeah, maybe busy drinking.

I don't feel bad that I'm saying no to this girl. Intrigue is a big vice for me. Hutch is a bigger one and I haven't had a drink in a few hours. As she pulls out a wad of bills I remember money trumps all.

"-I'll do it." Which is what I was going to end my sentence with all along. Can't get hutch if I don't have money.

"Gracias, gracias" She's so ecstatic. She almost drops the money which I quickly catch. "My name is Maria Rodriguez." She said before I could ask.

"And your brother?" I ended up having to ask.

"Jesús Rodriguez." Great, those names won't be hard to track. That's sarcasm.

The girl leaves and I go back to sleep thirsty.

3

"Nightmare!" That night I wake up screaming that one word. This is what happened's when I go sleep without going to the blackouts. Which is something I forgot to mention and becomes the seventh thing to know about moi. I live with it and don't talk about explaining it.

Rubbing my non swollen eye I look around for a liquor bottle that's not empty to help me forget what woke me up.

Despite not having found one I'm still in good spirits. This is an unusual trait for me. Perhaps it's because I have a large sum of money in my back pocket. A large bump as if a giant bee stung me in the backside.

This cheeriness starts to fade quickly once I realize why I have the money, work. I then put my new found money in the safest place I know, my shoes.

I have absolutely no idea where to begin. Do I just walk up to the closest junkie, there are a lot of them in this neighborhood. Then ask them 'excuse me, who is the local heroin drug kingpin?'

So I went to the downstairs apartment, a known drug den. I knocked on the door and asked the first guy who opened up. "Excuse me, do you know the guy who provided you with all your drugs, you know, the local drug kingpin?"

Needless to say I got a punch in the face. At least I didn't feel it. The force did knock me off my feet. After the encounter I walk outside. The first stop would have to be the morgue. I want to see the body before the sister takes it.

I'm going to the local hospital where the kid was taken. I head to the basement and open the door to the morgue. There is a desk and the man behind it is reading a newspaper and eating a donut. He doesn't react to me.

I walk up to the desk, "hey how you doing? I was looking for a body. You a mortician?"

He answers without looking up at me. "No, I'm the night shift guy and you're not supposed to be here." He still had part of the donut in his mouth.

"Yeah, I realize that, but I need to see the body. I'm a Marlowe, and the sister of the deceased wants me to look into his death."

"You got I.D.?" He asks, still not taking his eyes off his paper.

I don't have I.D. I know at this point none of my bullshit is going to work. So I'm in a fucking Sophie's Choice predicament here. Do I part with one of my children?

I take in a deep breath and let it out. "No, but Benjamin Franklin does." I say as I slip it on the desk over his paper. "It just so happened's to be money."

He examines it looking for the watermark and such. Then he puts it in his pocket. "My favorite President."

"This is why you work the night shift in the basement of a hospital looking after stiffs." I don't react until the last syllable leaves my lips. I'm thinking this is due to my lack of a filter. Luckily he doesn't notice, probably too busy gloating in his recent economic rise.

I go back to being disgusted by his previous statement. I then roll my eye. I know he won't come up for air from reading to catch that either. This whole exchange starts to pain me.

"Who you looking for?" He asks $100 richer.

"Jesús Rodriguez." I tell him now reeling from the separation anxiety.

He moves his paper to reveal a clipboard with a list of names on it. "No such name on the list." He goes back to reading.

That doesn't make sense because I know the ambulance took him here. It's the closest hospital to where he died. There's nothing else for miles. I'm standing there with my arms crossed and hand up to my mouth. It's time to zone. My thinking position. I'll do that shit in the middle of the street. It's like I'm in a trance.

Why would his name not be on there? If they didn't take his body here, then where? Maybe their stealing bodies and using them for experiments? No that doesn't make sense.

"Can I see the list," I ask. Maybe they misspelled his name. He looks up at me. Doesn't say anything, I know what he's thinking. He's thinking if I want to peek he'll need another note from his 'favorite President'. I furrow my brow "fuck that!" I quickly pull his newspaper up and grab the clipboard.

He doesn't make a move just goes back to reading.

I start looking at the list. Can't find the name anywhere. There's about fifty of them. Not even a misspelled version of the name.

There are three John Doe's though. Going with a hunch, "can I see these three?"

He reluctantly takes me to see three bodies that are located in three different rooms. The first one is tall and white, not him. The second was black. As soon as the zipper started to go down, I immediately said no. He was clearly annoyed.

With the third body I started feeling defeated as soon as the body bag came rolling out of its mini fridge. Wasn't until he started unzipping it that I noticed it was Jesús Rodriguez.

The clerk left the room as he says "don't fuck it."

I kept thinking why is he a John Doe? Did his sister with the rack not pick him up? She could have just known about his death from the TV. Maybe because she was so distraught it caused her not to want to claim his body? It's something to remember.

His body hadn't been examined. Most likely they just deemed it an O.D. Then they didn't need to. I look at his one track mark on his right arm. Just one, he didn't have any marks anywhere else.

She claimed he was a junkie but there would be a history of marks. Unless there in some hidden spots. Someone, me, could argue that if he had done them somewhere else on his body why do the one where anyone could see? It's possible there are some in say, the balls, but I am not checking there.

It's also possible he had one hit. That's all that was needed, like with a speedball. Why be on the roof if it's his first time? Seclusion, he wants to try it on his own without anyone looking or making comments? Problem is if it was his first time it negates what the sister said about him being a druggie.

Also, on his left shoulder is what looks like a similar tattoo to what his sister had. Now I can see the whole thing. It's a giant X, in the spaces are letters. Top space is a D. To the right is an E. The bottom is an A. The left part is filled with another D. It spells out DEAD.

After finishing up with the body I went to the quaint little bathroom in the basement of the hospital. Along with the humming florescent light flicking above me, I clean myself. In the mirror is a battered face with a swollen eye staring back at me.

My thoughts are deep but not about my jigsaw face. The body has the same tattoo as the sister. They look like gang tattoos.

Based on the fact there similar on two separate people. Plus, in the way there so crudely made. Why, were they in the same gang? The sister didn't know the leader's name, out of embarrassment? This is becoming quite a noodle scratcher.

I leave the hospital. While walking towards the bus to go home unfulfilled, some guy bumps into me. It knocks me to the side. I turn around to give him a clever quip when I notice he's already turned around staring at me.

He says "You are being watched, by Hermano de Sangre," then he walks away. The inside of his left forearm is the tattoo.

What the hell? I can't even pronounce that if I wanted to. Takes me a second to realize what that translates to, 'Brother' and 'Blood'. Sounds like this Blood guy might be connected to this gang. Maybe he's the leader. Even possibly this drug lord.

Have to do more research on that. Sounds like a real over dramatic douche though. What is this a comic book? Wouldn't be surprised if he had a lair.

Ugh, all this work is making me thirsty. I can only keep my quench in check for so long. I need to go to a place that can help me forget about this crap. Someplace where I can do my version of 'unwinding'. I suddenly get an idea but it requires me to do a bit of traveling to a better neighborhood.

I arrive at Pseudonym, it's a literary bar. A place where sophisticated nerds can go sit around a giant table drinking Pinot Grigio while discussing Dostoyevsky. There's a fireplace and bookshelves stacked with books that have twenty dollars' words inside them.

This doesn't seem like the kind of bar I would really associate with. I'm not the kind of barfly that stays with one place. I am no Norm; I do not have a Cheers. Frankly nor would I want one.

The variety of the bar, the better. It equals to more of a distraction for people to not interact with me. I do not want friends, but sometimes I do like making enemies.

I may seem like a traditional guy but sometimes you need something a little different in your drinking hole. Don't get me wrong, there are time when all I want is a dank, dark, empty, shithole. Other times I want something a bit flashier.

I especially like going here. Because it's fun to fuck with the patrons. Like when I ask one of them how it feels knowing Twilight has sold more copies than all of Charles Dickens novels put together. I'm sure that's not true, but it's amusing to see their faces squirm in disgust.

Another good thing about this place is the mini trivia game that's gets you a free drink if you win. It involves the give or take forty framed pictures of authors displayed around the bar.

You need to be able to guess ten names as well as a title of their work. The prize can be any drink. Since I enjoy trivia but not as much as I enjoy free booze, I play every time I come here. Let it be noted that's not very often.

Usually the average amount of people who come here can't do it. Which it seems like the so-called intellectuals who do show up should be able to. It's not irony that they can't. The simple fact is that most who come here are full of shit much like most so-called intellectuals.

So I will give them the answers provided they give me half the prize. I'll state to them if they order let's say, a gin and tonic, they take the water whereas I will take the gin. That doesn't bode over well. I end up just pouring half in my cup.

It isn't a very easy test; a lot of the pictures aren't of the most common authors. Of course you will see the king of mandatory high school reading, Bill Shakespeare. There's also the underappreciated Vonnegut, Wright, and Dahl. The best is the picture of Pynchon, nobody knows what the hell he looks like.

Getting the identity is half the battle but also the hardest bit. Once you get that the titles pretty much come to you.

Plus, the bartenders and servers rarely seem to notice that I barely pay for drinks. That my glass is always half full with random liquids. When they do I get warned and then eventually kicked out. I'll come back a few weeks later and it will start all over again. For a place that's owned by a member of MENSA they sure are dumb.

After I get caught this time I'm escorted out. This was my version of fun, drinking for free despite having money. My way of relaxing before I delve back into this clusterfuck of a case. I head home not even close to the blackouts. I'll have some unfinished business back at my place.

When I get off the bus and walk to my building I make a plan. I'm going to call my connection at a nearby precinct to get more information. Every Marlowe's got one. Don't want to go there in person for reasons that are my own.

I make it up to my floor with my eyes down on the ground. I don't see the hand that comes at me and smacks me in the mouth. My lip's still a little swollen from what was it, yesterday?

What happened's when it gets hit all over again, I'm going to find out. So who hit me now? Who has sent my head back? Making me touch my lip to see if I have blood dripping down my face?

"I want my money!" The Indo-Guyanese dickhead standing in front of me adjusting his rings that just popped my mouth is none other than Derek Powers. The slumlord extraordinaire.

He stands at about 5' 10". His black hair is slicked back with enough grease to get an elephant through an anthill. The white suit he's wearing emphasizes his dark skin.

This is the opposite for his smiling pearly whites. They practically glow due to being accentuated by his goatee. His look says a lot about his personality. That he thinks very highly of himself.

It also represents that he's overcompensating with what he really thinks, that he's similar to the dirt he walks on. That's the only think I'll ever agree with him on.

This guy owns a bunch of buildings in the area. Most are rock dens with very few families. He always seems to get his money in the end. "Why don't you collect from the A-list tenants from downstairs? I'm sure they can pay you in rocks."

"Shut up deadbeat." I now have a pretty good idea of who left that artwork on my door. "They will get theirs only worry for yourself."

"You know; I must not have noticed your Lincoln outside. You hide it from the junkies afraid they'll defecate on it?" I've seen it happen.

"Stop changing the subject. You owe me money deadbeat. Two months. You no pay, you no have fingers. No one would dare shit on my car." This is true I have never seen druggies shit on his. Just other peoples.

I take one shoe off, take out the wad and give it to him. I exhale, "fine, two months suck on it." Goodbye my beauties. The other half is in my other shoe. Dickhead leaves walking past me. I turn and ask him, "Hey, have you ever heard of Hermano de Sangre?"

As he's counting his money he answers rather gruffly "Fuck You."

I open the door to my office. Powers has left a considerable amount of bad taste in my mouth. Tastes like battery acid. I'm thinking about how I never did solve the mystery of Derek. Here come the W&H questions again. How connected is he? Whose he connected with? How much does he own? How can I get a piece of it?

I've never committed any time to finding out the answer. Frankly, I've been too hutch faced to care. That makes me sad and parched.

The inside of my office consists of a couch, a desk, a smelly bathroom, and some windows. This is pretty much where I've lived since I lost my apartment. I don't know when or how, maybe a fire? Another mystery to solve.

The bad experience I've just lived through has turned me off from calling in my faceless hook up. Besides it's too late to annoy her now. I decide to finish off the buzz I was trying to create before. I find half a bottle and let it do its thing. I am shortly introduced to the blackouts.

4

I wake up groggy. I rarely have hangovers, but I do feel like I only slept for a short amount of time. I stumble my way to the phone.

I have a landline. I don't own a cellphone, a rare occurrence in this era. I can't afford one nor do I want one. I try to be as disconnected as possible. I have a computer in the office. It's so old it might as well be a Commodore; I think it might be.

I pick up the receiver. I own one of those old phones when they were still made of metal. The kind you would find in an office. The number gets dialed and I talk to my contact at the precinct, Sarah, she's a faceless.

"What do you want?" This is what I hear after her formal greeting.

"To hear your lovely voice, to reminisce about the good times, to catch up on current times-"

"Bullshit! You want something! You still owe me money you know?" She interrupts me bringing to my attention that I seem to owe a lot of people money. "Besides, there weren't that many good times." That has to be a lie, just to get a rise out of me. It doesn't work.

"Fine, we will skip the pleasantries. I need something from you, a favor. I'll owe you."

"You already owe me a lot." Which we've already established. "Frankly you owe me enough." There's silence and then her voice drifts back, "what do you want?" This time she says it in a way that isn't so much harsh and unwelcoming. More defeated and sympathetic.

"I need a background check. Jesús Rodriguez, M, early twenties. Brown hair, 5'10". With a tattoo on the left shoulder."

"Do you know how broad of a search that is? There's probably enough to fill up a whole neighborhood!"

"I know," I respond. "Try your best." I hang up before she could curse me out.

After the phone call I sit there tired and bored. Mostly bored. What's the best thing to do when you're bored, drink! I know I'm out of any supply. I decide to spend some well-earned cash. I leave my office being extra careful looking behind every corner so I don't get a surprise pop.

I go shopping at the local liquor store where they know me by name. As I'm coming back I'm so full of glee about my new purchase I was distracted and didn't look around the corner. This Rockface jumped out with a blade in his hands.

"Give me the fucking money, I know you got some." How could he know that I wonder? "Come one come on, it's in your shoe I know it! I followed you from your place!"

Fucking Powers, I bet he tipped off this smelly fuck that I had money. My other bet is that he had an idea that I had more in my other shoe. What kind of world do we live in that we can't trust our landlords?

At this point I've had it. These past few days I've been kicked around so much more than normal. I haven't cared. There was no reason to. This dick wants my money and possibly my hutch. No one gets in-between me and my drinky drink.

This is a learning process. By that I mean I have forgotten there are much more things to learn, about me. I'm not some hutch jockey shmuck who one day decided to be a hutch jockey shmuck. I had a life and in that life I wouldn't let creeps like this get the best of me. I can take care of myself. I just choose not to for my own reasons.

Secret piece of info number eight, Captain Thunder. I'm speaking of course of the handbook, 'How to be like Captain Thunder. It's based on a comic book character. He was my hero growing up. I wanted to be him so bad when I was a kid. It has real techniques in it. Things like how to throw a punch, how make a punch, how to deflect a gunshot.

Not the bullet itself, more like deflecting the gun before the shot.

I live by this book, as hokey as it sounds. It is my bible and my teacher. I have studied it through and through. There's even a part on how to survey a crime scene. Or how to be perceptive. A good chunk of what I've learned in life came from this book. There's one chapter in there that I'd like to take the literal page from today, how to disarm a knife.

Rockface is only standing a foot away. He's so strung out I doubt he knows what's he's doing. The trick is similar with disarming a gun is to move your body away.

To the right as you grab his arm pushing it away or up. With the free hand hitting the inside of his elbow that connects the fore and upper arm. I do this quickly and surprisingly with no effort. I was sluggish than I used to be. He was just slower.

Rockface moans and it brings him to his knees. I finish it off by head-butting him. I'm too excited to start analyzing more into why this guy attacked me. I know it was Powers, he'll get his. I go off on my merry way, trying really hard not to skip. I'm anticipating that sweet, sweet liquor.

I don't know what time it is. A watch is something else I don't own. Another sign of how disconnected I am with society. It's been a long night. I go back to the office. Like a kid opening a present on Christmas morning I am excited as I open my bottle. All that's left is drinking and sleeping, eventually.

5

I'd like to think alcoholism is a parasite or a leech that attaches itself to you. It's attracted to sadness, to desperation. You're not born with it. The leech comes looking for you. They say you never know you have a problem until you hit rock bottom. I don't know what those words mean. 'Rock bottom', more like quitting.

Back at my place the phone rings, I slowly open my eyes squinting to reveal the sun blaring in my retinas. I answer the phone, its Sarah. "Didn't I just call you?" I asked confused.

"That was two days ago." Sheesh, I must have had a good time. "You haven't changed." She said with an attitude.

"Why would I?" I asked.

She ignored me. "I looked into your name, Jesús Rodriguez. There are 97 of them in the city."

"How many of them are still alive? Meaning has any of them died in the past week?"

She exhales out of annoyance. "I don't know, some of these are dead. I don't know when they died."

"How many of them have kicked it?"

"Give me a minute." I wait, "ten of them."

I'm about to say something I don't want to. She isn't going to like this either. "I need all of their info."

"Jesus I am busy. I can't spend all day with you on the phone!"

She's pissed. So am I. I don't want to call all these people. I don't want to go door to door either. "Sarah, I'm going to say something you never hear me say, please. Now you know it's serious."

There was a pause. "You know, there was a time-"

I interrupt her. "Would you shut up?" I'm annoyed. "Jesus, you gotta ruin our moment. You finally had me begging. Well fuck it now, I don't care. Do what you want!"

More silence, "you have a pen, you better write this shit down."

For ten minutes she tells me all ten last address and last known phone numbers. Every time I write down another number or letter I dread how I'm going to have to talk to so many people.

After she gave me everything I wanted to ask her. "One more thing Sarah."

I start to become uncharacteristically nervous due to the fact that I know I am going to butcher this name. Maybe she won't notice. "I know you don't work in the Anti-Gang unit or Narcotics, but have you ever heard of Hermano de Sangre?"

A moment of silence is created. "There has been talk around the precinct of a Hermano de Sangre," she says it perfectly.

"Apparently he's the leader of some big drug crew. They've been trying to connect him to over a dozen murders. As well as head of this distribution crew that's been operating for over a year now. Of course, no one knows what he looks like, or who he is. Some say he covers his identity. Loved your pronunciation by the way," Damn it!

Then she starts to get suspicious, "why the hell you asking?"

"No real reason, just for a case." Do not want to give much away.

"Uh-huh, are you still doing jobs for lollipops?" She's asks no longer curious about my sniffing around.

"It wasn't for just any lollipop; it was a Blow Pop. That has bubble gum in them. By the way, what's the name of this gang he runs?" I think I know the answer already.

"What," she gets pulled out of her daydreaming. "Oh, their called The Dead. Again it's mostly just speculation and theory. They have a gang tattoo. It's a big X with letters in it. Never understood that. Why not just tattoo 'I did it' on your forehead it makes it easier."

It's zoning time. "Ok, thanks." My mind starts to drift away. I don't even notice I just said the one word I don't like saying, other than 'please', 'thanks.'

"Hey, you owe me-" Click.

They're called 'The Dead'. How stupid, but I shouldn't be surprised. Talk about theatrics though. So both siblings were in this gang. Something the sister didn't mention, why? Also, now it's somewhat official and we have a name for this kingpin.

Now I have to work on the dead kid's name. So first I call the morgue. It's been a few days and I want to know if the sister claimed the body yet. It hasn't been claimed. The morgue can hold a body indefinitely depending on the circumstances.

This is being considered an O.D., a real open and shut case. Plus, there's overcrowding. So their only going to hold on to the body for two more days. I hang up with them and start to wonder why she hasn't claimed it yet.

Got to write down all these questions for her. If and when I see her again. They're starting to pile up.

I start begrudgingly calling the numbers on my list. I upset a lot of people reopening up the wounds of lost ones. Out of the ten, six picked up. Three hung up on me and three cursed me out. That leaves me with four who didn't pick up. I'll go looking tomorrow. All this detective work has made me tired and thirsty.

6

I wake up the next morning dragging myself over to the phone to call the morgue again. I figure I'm going to need a picture of the smelly body to show the four numbers that didn't pick up yesterday.

The morgue then informs me; the body is gone. Apparently shortly after I called someone stole the body. They can't tell me who. Is someone on my trail? Better question, why am I talking in a first person narrative to ask myself questions?

I decide to go visit the addresses without the picture. This takes all day. Out of the four places; two slammed doors, one grandmother crying uncontrollably, and the last place looked abandoned.

Even though I didn't have the picture I just asked them when their Jesús died. Also if they already claimed the body, that sort of thing. Normally they're not terribly insensitive questions. Coming out this face of ennui though, hell, I'd slam the door in my face too.

As I walk down the stairs from the brownstone that was abandoned I notice a man across the street. He's staring at me. He looks familiar. Kinda like that guy who bumped into me in the street. He just stares. I start walking towards him. I have to wait for the busy cars zooming by so I could cross.

Then I notice a white van speeding out of my peripheral vision. It passes the guy. Just like something out of a fucking movie, the guy disappears! What the hell did I stumble into?

I'm finally back to my building. Walking up the stairs I realize, I smell. I mean it's been a few days since I showered right? I don't know why I'm asking myself. I get distracted though.

Who just happened to be in my hallway outside my door, the innocent angel, Maria.

"Oh seńor, seńor." She starts bellowing while wearing another low cut drop top. This one is hiding her tattoo. Mascara is once again running down her face. The aroma of cinnamon soon fills my lungs.

"Oh no, no, no, no," I interrupt her. "You listen lady, I got questions for you. I really need to know was your brother right handed?"

I give her the chance to answer, "Si, Si I think so." Interesting answer since it doesn't fit with what I saw on the body.

It came pouring out after that. "Good, now why didn't you mention that you two were in the same gang?

Also, where is your brother's body? Who the hell is Hermano de Sangre," I'm starting to get better at saying his name. "Finally why is he following me?" I don't know if that's all of them. Damn, I should have written them down.

All of a sudden her eyes widen. She stops crying, "no, Hermano de Sangre, El Diablo, El Diablo!"

She starts freaking out. She's screaming and runs off down the stairs. Am I supposed to be scared of this guy? Everyone is so dramatic. I go in my office and try to relax. Trying to mull some things over.

So she's scared. I get it, scary kingpin guy. Why be in the gang? Forced, maybe sexually? She's young, good looking, meek and easily manipulated. Maybe in exchange for legal status?

All this deduction gets me thirsty. I look around for a drink with no prevail. Thus I go back outside to get some drinky drink. While buying the hutch I'm happy.

I am once again in the mood to skip as I leave the liquor store. It all comes crashing down when I notice the van. It appears in the corner of my eye again. I'm sure that weirdo kid is near-ACK!

7

Time has no meaning with a black hood over your head. Seconds seem like minutes, which can stretch into feeling like hours. The darkness plays games with your mind that way. There is only emptiness. Except you have your other senses to focus and rely on. Panic can seep in and ruin that concentration.

My Captain Thunder training had taught me to be aware of my surroundings at all times. This instance would be perfect to use it. To be able to listen and mentally catalogue any significant sound. So I can then go back and be able to piece together where I'm going and how I can get back there.

I guess I would normally try to do this. To be honest though, the only sound I'm focusing on is the one I heard before I came in here. I am currently stewing in my anger from it. When whoever it was that came up from behind, bagged me and shoved me in this white van.

I'm assuming it was the white van. I'm also assuming it was that weird kid that's been following me that bagged me. That noise by the way that pissed me off was the sound of my liquor bottle smashing on the ground when they grabbed me.

With me being distracted I couldn't tell how long we were on the road or any distinctive sounds on the way. Now we've stopped. Their aggressively rushing me out and placing me somewhere. The smells are immense and they come from all over. They are so variously random, from car oil, to food, cologne, and burning wax?

My hood gets slipped off me. I still have to squint despite it being dark in here. I'm on my knees, hands tied behind my back. I'm in a giant empty warehouse. There's candle everywhere. In the left corner on the other side of the warehouse is a giant of a man. His back is to everything, just staring at the wall.

His hands are behind him. A guy goes over and whispers in his ear. Who is also holding my hood. He starts to slowly turn his head to the left to look at me. He turns around as his body faces me. He's huge, has to be close to seven feet tall.

Looks like he works out every day too. He's wearing a black suit. His head is bald, and his face is painted with a red skull. Aww fuck, I'm in a goddamn lair!

He starts walking towards me. The situation starts to become obvious to me. There's a fucking altar, for

Santeria or some shit. A giant pentagram painted, what in blood, on the middle of the floor. Gimme a fucking break with this shit! The skull painted on him, it's supposed to be blood. With the effect of dripping off of his face.

The way he walks, slow, heel to toe, heel to toe. With each step he slowly swings his shoulder. It's like a wrestler's entrance done slowly. In fact, he looks like a Mexican wrestler, on rock. He stands there with his back in and chest out playing for fear, a shit load of it.

He is not going to get that here. I must have a surprised look on my face, based on the crap that's developing in front of me. This can be misconstrued as fear.

He squats in front of me, "you know me. I. Am. Hermano. De. Sangre." He says as he stares at me with his red eyes created by contacts.

In his accent he emphasizes the word 'blood'. He starts his sentences in a loud tone but sometimes ends them in a whisper. He speaks as if he should be greeting vacationers to a mysterious isle filled with imagination.

So of course with all this I can't help but laugh. "HAHAHAHAHAHA!" Just a big roar from the bottom of my gut. Practically in his face. I haven't laughed like this in, ever.

This angers Blood. Just thinking about his dumb name makes me chuckle. He doesn't appreciate how I find him delightfully hilarious. So he counter's this by smacking me. "Your laughter disrespects me!"

The open backhand jerks me to the right. I spit out blood and I could taste it. The whack has stopped me from laughing. It hasn't turned it into crying or panic, just anger. He doesn't seem to notice that though.

"The aroma you have created, it is shit. You have shit yourself from fear." As he stands this gets his goons who are nearby to laugh.

I answer calmly, "no, actually it's because I haven't showered in three days." I realize that this excuse, although the truth is not much better than the alternative.

"Yes, fear from my presence! Fear from the knowledge that I will kill you!" He says with his arms out making him look like a giant T. Someone is being obtuse.

I try again. "No, see, me no shower, me now stinky. I don't know if you could understand that from where you come from." Look, I'm not racist. I hate everyone equally. It's just, I wanted to get a rise out of him. Hell, I don't know where he comes from. It's possible however wherever that is, it doesn't have indoor plumbing.

It doesn't matter though. The insult falls on deaf ears. "Are you the Darkstar?"

Who, Darkstar, who the fuck is that now? Another moron with a Lucha Libre fetish? I tried to explain, "I don't know what the fuck you are talking about!"

To no prevail, "Sí, you are the Darkstar! You are the one who is stepping into my domain. You are the one who blew up my warehouse, my plant. You are the one who has become the thorn in my side for weeks." Wow, he really is the next Sherlock Holmes. I don't think I could even try to convince this meathead that I am not who he thinks I am.

He starts exploring the conclusion on his own. "You are the one who has shit himself in Hermano de Sangre's presence."

"I did not shit myself", I yell as I try to defend myself again. "Jesus, you would think you could tell the difference between shit and just really bad B.O."

He ignored me once again his over acting continues. "You are not the Darkstar. The one who has bested me at every turn would not come here and shit himself based on my intimidating presence."

"Are you fucking serious," I yell out. No one seems to notice my outburst. He's going on and on, it's making me sick. I'm the only one who seems to notice this is ridiculous.

I'm starting to think everyone else is in some sort of trance. Reminds me of a cult. He walks back and forth spewing his monologue. I roll my good eye back. I act and feel like a bored child. My legs are getting numb.

"No," he yells as he goes on, "you must work for the Darkstar. An errand boy, a peon. Listen to me then peon, you will tell me where Darkstar is!" He squats down again and gets in my face. "I do not care who he is. I only care where. So I may squash him like the bug he is, you understand?" Am I in a Bond movie?

He gets up again when someone comes from behind me and cuts the rope tied behind my hands. Blood is watching and smiling as the same person takes my coat off.

Then my shirt sleeve gets rolled up and my right arm pulled out. Blood takes a cigar out of his pocket and starts to light it. I know where this is going and it's going to be a comedy of errors.

"The cigar is like a woman." He says as he goes to puff his phallic device that for some reason reminds him of a woman. "You must treat it well, carefully, making sure it doesn't break. You must nurture it so it can bloom into something beautiful."

"So, let me get this straight." I say as Blood's goon holds my arm tight. "A cigar, is nothing like a woman because that is the worst fucking analogy I have ever heard. You basically described everything. How is anything you just said not relatable to any process?"

Once again, he is swept up in his own soliloquy. "Yes, just like a woman." He smiles as he pulls the cigar away from his mouth looking at the butt. He then takes the cigar that's in-between his first and middle finger and moves it in and out of his mouth. Sucking on the cigar.

"Yeah, just like a woman." I repeated, but much more sarcastic.

Blood once again squats in front of me as he starts to smoke. "Pain is for the weak. Pain stops a man from achieving his goals. With pain one can never persevere through the toughest goals that life throws at us. The heroes are the ones of us who look at pain and without so much as a flinch keep going."

"They say 'not today or any other day pain, you will not make me your slave.' When we finished our objectives and later in life if we look back can we honestly say 'I did this in the face of pain'? If so, then that is a true accomplishment. This makes you a man and even in death, this makes you a winner."

I guess that means I'm a real man and a hero because this is not going to go well, for him.

With the cigar out of his mouth he holds it over my arm. "You will tell me where the Darkstar is. He will not destroy me. He is only slowing me down when he blew up my warehouse. He will never destroy me. Never destroy my empire! Ha-ha-," he yells this last part.

"Would you just get this over with already?" I interrupt him. Again he mentioned that 'warehouse' of his. I'm assuming this was some sort of distribution plant or something to do with drugs.

"Your valor is invigorating my friend. Let us begin." He pushes the lit part of the extension of his penis onto my arm at the top of my forearm. I have no reaction. "Hahaha, it burns you, all the way to your soul!!!!" He stops, "tell me what I want to know."

"You're an asshole! A theater major who couldn't hack it in the real world. Maybe you were so bullied because you were a fairy for being a theater major. Then you decided to get revenge by being a WWE reject!"

"Round two my friend," he ignores everything and again puts the cigar onto my arm while he yells. "Tell me, tell me your secrets! Pour your guts about your leader! A leader who you have sworn an oath to, but will yield because you are in pain! It is the most agonizing pain in your life!" I am so bored, I yawned as Sir Laurence Olivier went on.

I guess he too got bored with the 'torture'. "Your courage in the sight of death, humbles me. It makes me respect you. This is what I do, because Hermano de Sangre cares. You are now one of mine. You will go back to the

Darkstar. When you do my men will be there."

I had drifted off a bit. Blood's goon woke me up when he grabbed my arm and pulled me into a standing position. I was in that state between being awake and just hitting the subconscious. While my eyes were half open I was questioning myself about something.

That's the perfect instant to come up with great ideas the problem has always been remembering such thoughts. My issue is I'm always too inebriated to even have such a moment.

Before I could be shuffled back into the van I snap out of my drowsiness. "Wait one more thing, how the hell did you find me? What made you even follow me?" I ask the burning question that bothered me as I was slipping into sleepytown.

"One of the men saw you on the television. Hermano de Sangre saw something in you, had you followed. You provided the address. That was pretty estupido gringo."

I start to think that his explanation sounds like utter bullshit and there's more to it as I say to myself, "whatever."

The hood comes back on and I get escorted back into the van. They drop me off in front of my building. I go to where they first picked me up. I mourn the broken bottle of hutch I dropped.

I then realize I have got to get to the hospital thanks to that ahole. If I don't get this cigar burn looked at it could get infected. I wouldn't even know if it did until it smells. On my way to the hospital, then to the morgue.

These events start to make me think about what it was like growing up with not being able to feel pain. I had many trips to the hospital. I had a bad accident at school and not knowing at first made it worse. My mother freaked out and forbid me with playing sports. That limited my social life growing up.

My mom was my best friend and not by choice. I had been in and out of hospitals for major injuries so much when I was younger that the state investigated my parents. They thought I was being abused. If I was only that lucky. They had a hard time explaining that my condition made it easy for any wound to get worse before they could notice it.

That's why my mother came up with the ritual of checking my body for cuts, bruises, or breaks every night before bed. I still try to do it today. When I'm not too drunk. It was instilled in me. I hate admitting it was a good idea my mother had. Despite hating doing it my whole life. Everyone has one good idea, except Hitler.

I get to the emergency room. A doctor patches me up. I got pissed at the comment the doctor makes as he's fixing me. "Are you a self-mutilator?" All the fucking nerve! How dare he look down at me. Even if I did have a problem, only I can do that to people!

I tell him, "The burn is on my right arm. I'm a righty, so how could I have possibly done that to myself?" It could only be done if you're a righty. The probability of a righty doing something like that with his left is-

Holy shit, that kid, Jesús. I had completely forgotten. His sister says he was a righty. If he was given the hit of Heroin and it wasn't self-inflicted that contradicts with what was on his body. There's no way he would have been able to tie one off on his right arm then. He wasn't alone, someone had to be up there with him. Whether it was friend or foe that remains to be seen.

I'm officially changing this case from a suicide to a homicide. Not that anyone gives a fuck what I think. Except the client. Who I don't fully trust. As long as she keeps giving me money though I don't give a shit.

As I leave the hospital I come up with the idea to go someplace where I can think and mull this new information over. So I pick a bar. I also want to let off some steam. I'm pretty pissed due to this new information.

The bar I'm heading to, the Triple Crown, is a new establishment. From what I've heard it has a horse race theme to it. They specialize in Triple Crown winners, all twelve of them.

When I get there it is not what I expected. Extravagant, expensive looking murals with jockeys and horses surround the whole place. Sections are dedicated to the winners each with a framed picture. All the patrons are dressed for the Kentucky Derby and drinking mint juleps. I am disappointed since I thought this would be decorated more like a track. Filled with cigar smoke, ripped losing tickets on the floor, noisy, and packed.

This nor the snobbish presence stop me from sitting at the bar and throwing back a few, or six. The bartender takes, makes, and serves my order when I decide to ask him a question. "Where are the pictures of the losers and the glue and dog food factories they ended up in?" my comment falls on deaf ears.

It's a small distraction that quickly fades. Now I'm left to my thoughts about what's going on in this weak excuse of a case.

There was something Blood said that keeps ringing in my head. Among all the bullshit that was spewing from his painted up mouth. It was about his warehouse. The one that got blown up by Darkstar or so he thinks. Maybe there's something in that.

There's a group of young professional douchebags directly behind me at the bar. Their giggling breaks me out of my zoning. Which annoys me greatly. One of them decides to interact.

"Hey buddy, you ever heard of a shower?" Shortly after I hear the rest of the sowing circle laugh like a bunch of cheerleaders.

It's not the cleverly witty observation that stings the most, it's the interruption. That's the reason for what I do next. Swiveling my barstool around I get a good look at him. With a shot in my hand, I stare into his eyes as he waits for my response. I say, "Ever heard of an abortion? It's what your mother should have had." I then take my shot.

I spin back around as mister tough guy wants to look big in front of his group of the Hitler youth. "You mother fucker," he says in defiance as he wishes his friends hold him back.

I called this kid's bluff by giving his insult back to him. I know he won't expect what I do next. He hopes I'll turn yellow at the sight of his version of beating his chest.

Instead I slightly turn my stool just enough to reach the bar, but not enough that my eyes aren't still locked with his. I slam my closed fist still holding the shot glass onto the bar.

I reveal the bloody mess, take a jagged piece, and proceed to slowly cut the exposed part of my chest. I do this without unlocking my eye with his.

Needless to say, it causes all of them to have pee their pants shocked looks on their faces. As they practically run out of the bar I can't help but smile to myself. I was going to smash a bottle on my head without a reaction on my face. That would have been pretty stupid though.

I turn back around to the bar happy in my insanity as I immediately see the bartender yell in my face, "Get out!"

The end of that little excitement will lead me home without being too wasted for the blackouts. I will have to remedy that. People like that, bullies, they piss me off. I knew they wouldn't be tough enough to beat me up gang initiation style. That I could freak them out by showing them what the real world looks like, scary and gross.

Back at my place I drink the rest of my reserve until I get the blackouts.

8

Waking up the next day I try to fight back the grogginess. I pick up the phone to once again talk to my faceless connection Sarah.

"What now? I'm really fucking busy." She's so happy to hear from me again.

"I just need one more thing. Any warehouses in the city suddenly get blown up? Maybe just mysteriously caught on fire in the last few months?"

"Oh, let me look on my super cop computer. One moment please, bleep, bop, boop." Her attempt in pretending to be a computer.

"Ok, I'll wait." I don't get frustrated by her attempt at sarcasm, instead I play into it.

"Jesus call you later!" She hangs up the phone.

I start to check myself for any surprise cuts, bruises, or breaks since I've neglected doing it for a while.

People have asked me, 'What's your poison?'

'Anything to the equivalent of that.' I would usually answer. Although Rattlesnake Venom is good this time of year. Whatever time of year we're in right now.

There are so many different kinds of liquor with catchy brand names. 'Fireball', 'Dragon's Breath', 'Brimstone', or 'Satan's Queef'. As if these are supposed to draw you in alone. It works though, millions of shmucks buy them based on brand.

What I only care about is if it will get me to the blackouts. It could be hobo piss but if it's a 101 proof, I'll try it. Don't come to me about Wine either. That shit is for two kinds of people, Women and people who wear powdered wigs. Otherwise, why bother?

I start to close my eyes as I'm sitting up until I'm awoken by the telephone. I'm welcoming it. Hey, I can see out of the other eye finally. I pick up the phone, "huh"?

"Three known locations where there were warehouse fires in the last six months: 15 Ditko Street; 129 Castle Way; and 550 Byrne Ave; Leave me alone." -Click- She hung up.

After much procrastinating, I take a well sought after shower. It's more like a sink shower. I don't own a full bathroom. I do however change clothes.

I head to the first address 15 Ditko via bus. There's not much left of the building. It was located pretty much in a desolate neighborhood. Mostly other warehouses. Even during the day not much going. Some cars whizzing by at the nearest main road. I'm looking around. It's hard to find anything, most of the building is burned down. Anything still around is stained black. That smell the strong odor of stale burning still lingers in the air.

Not all of the building is gone as I previously thought. The bottom parts of the wall that are connected to the ground still remain although barely. Near the front where the main entrance might have been still has some graffiti on it.

The piece is cut off and I can only make out the bottom part. It looks familiar though. It's a triangle with the bottom part missing. With the letter A inside of it. Along with part of a D to the left and the bottom bit of an E to the right of it.

The Dead tattoo here as a tag. At my first shot too. I was worried I'd have to go to three different addresses.

I don't know what I was looking to find. I guess to validate the fact it did exist. Also that it looked like it could have been a drug den.

As I leave I pass an empty field. On the other side of the tall fences surrounding the field a homeless man pops up.

"That was a drug den you know." He says with his shit breath hitting me hard. I was surprised it didn't erode the metal fence as it passed through.

I'll play along, "What makes you say that?" I say playing the detective.

"What do you think I'm stupid? I may be a drunk, but I know a drug den when I see one. Constant back and forth during the middle of the night. Sometimes with tractor trucks. There were no signs on the building."

"Sometimes there would be this big guy, looked like a wrestler. He even had his face with paint or something." Blood, so maybe this cook isn't crazy.

"Then, one night there were these shadowy figures. They come out of the black, nothingness. They sneak into the building through the shadows. Then, BOOM, a blast of fire, knocked me on my ass. When I get up everything is gone, replaced with fire."

Maybe this guy isn't so 'sane' after all. I nod to him and start to walk away as he mutters to himself about 'the fire'. I take a few steps and realize I might have been looking into a future mirror. I take those steps back as destiny looms over me. I hand him some money. His glassy eyes move over to look into mine and he whispers, "thank you."

Back at my place I sit on my couch. I'm exhausted, not from fatigue, but mentally I'm spent.

Doesn't stop me from zoning about my present situation. I got a deceased kid, whose body is missing. Whose identity by the way cannot be found anywhere. His 'suicide' is starting to look like a homicide by the way of Hermano de Sangre. Who was also the leader of the gang he was in with his sister. I'm getting better at saying it.

Why kill him though? Where's the motive? Was he stealing contraband? Maybe he was connected to Darkstar. With the way his sister reacted to Blood's name it almost seems clear he's involved with the kid's death.

Speaking of the mysterious 'Darkstar' now I'm in the middle of some drug war between him and Blood. Who knew these drug lords' love their comic book villain codenames? I'm all over the place with this and can't get my bearings.

Suddenly, I get a hunch. I go outside and I'm right. Blood's white van is sitting outside my place. I walk up to it and the engine starts. I jump in front, "stop!" I yell hoping he won't hit the gas pedal and keep going. Luckily he doesn't.

I ask him to roll down the window, he does. It's the same kid who first bumped into me and has been following me. His eyes have a glaze to them. It's as if he sees me, but doesn't notice me.

"Look man, I need some info before I can reveal Darkstar. He's in hiding you know." I lie, terribly. "Do you know, Jesús Rodriguez?"

He stares at me like he doesn't know what to say. Maybe he can't do anything until Blood tells him. I'm convinced this is a cult and their brainwashed. I then try something. I hope he's as stupid as I think he is. "Hermano de Sangre told me I could ask anything I want as long as I produce the identity of Darkstar."

Time goes by. Seconds maybe. You could see the rat running in his wheel through this dipshit's eyeballs. This person is no longer a person in my book he's just a zombie.

It finally speaks. "I, do not know this name." I don't have a picture to show this numbnuts. Very stupid of me that I didn't get one. Still, he doesn't know this guy's name. Despite being in the gang.

I decided to switch gears. "What about the warehouse, it was a drug distribution center? Darkstar blew it up, right"?

He stares at me blankly. His eyes start to twitch. Almost as if he was having a conversation with Blood in his mind to see if he could answer.

Then his eyes widen as he spoke. "That was no drug distribution center. Hermano de Sangre is building an army." He exuberated with pride as he told me this. "That coward Darkstar, he tried to kill this army. He cannot stop what has already taken form. There is a war coming!" He said as he smiled.

"A war, against Darkstar?" I asked thinking I already know the answer.

"No," he scoffs, I guess I didn't. "Darkstar is a cucaracha that we will exterminate. He and his Fearless Five."

"No the real target is someone else, someone bigger. The puppet master Hermano de Sangre calls him. Los Muertos led by Hermano de

Sangre will reach up and grab his strings! With his mighty scissors cut the lifeline from which was forged onto him."

He grabs the steering wheel tight, looks up at the van's ceiling and starts yelling. "He will be free!! We are Los Muertos, you cannot kill which is already-" This all becomes very creepy and uncomfortable. Everyone around us in the street are looking.

I stop him in mid-sentence, "yeah, I get it because you're already dead." I roll my eyes. This is great, more players in this crappy story called my life. "Who are the Fearless Five?" I ask not really wanting to know.

"They are all cobardes. They follow Darkstar. They will fall by the blade too." Or scissors apparently.

"OK, who is the 'puppet master'?"

"I do not know. All I know is what Hermano de Sangre tells me. That the puppet master is a scourge."

Are all of these people so melodramatic? When you join this gang, do you have to join a local theater group or something? "Ok, good. You can tell your boss; I think I got it." That's a lie, "and I'll set up a meeting tomorrow."

I start to walk away. The engine starts on the white van. As it drives off from behind me, there's a crash and a scream. I quickly walk over to it.

He drove up on the sidewalk and smashed into a mailbox. I look into the driver's side window where I just had that eloquent conversation. There I see the man who unknowingly became my informant. He's clutching his throat with his eyes widen. His mouth opens with a terrified look on his face which has turned red.

As I move my fingers closer to his neck to see if there's a pulse, I hear a click. It's more like an ignition. A spark of fire starts to come out of his mouth. I pull my hand back and in a second his entire face engulfs in a blaze.

It starts catching fire inside the van. The flames start to become too big for me to handle so I push myself away. I'm yelling at people to move. The flame that started off as a spark has now turned into a fire that has consumed the whole inside.

I hear a motorcycle nearby. From the sidewalk I look past the smoke and flame that used to be a motor vehicle. I see someone dressed in a one piece all black leather motorcycle suit. The face is hidden by the helmet with the fire reflecting in the visor. Then suddenly veering off, fast.

I watch as the firefighters try to put this mess out. I'm finding it hard to piece everything together in my mind. The faceless men come and I skedaddle. I don't like them. Besides, I'm too involved to lie.

I hardly doubt anyone will be able to recount my chat with the recently deceased. I sit in my office and reflect. I start shaking my head in disbelief from my reflection. What the fuck did I just witness? What is this James Bond bullshit?

The weight of what is going on in my head has spread to my eyes. As hard as I try my eyes just can't take this drama anymore. My eyelids have become Atlas, my problems the globe. Atlas is losing. It's lost.

9

I wake up the next day in a sweat. Due to the fact that I dozed off without drinking. I leave the office to remedy that. The sun beats down on me as I walk to the liquor store. I don't care what time it is. I want to sleep without waking up freaked out like I bombed a small village in Vietnam.

As I get to the corner a white van drives up on the sidewalk. I get a surreal sense of Deja vu wash over me. A man gets out who could be a relation to the guy whose face melted off yesterday.

"Hermano de Sangre wants to see you," is all he says as a black hood gets put over my head.

Later at Blood's lair he is once again standing in the back not facing me. He spins around, I can tell he's pissed. His yelling confirms it.

"Your time is up. Where is my meeting with the Darkstar?"

"I didn't have enough time." I say as I do a bad job of pretending to care.

"You also had a man of mine killed."

"Now wait a minute," I say as I try to defend myself. "His head blowing off was not my fault."

"But it was you who interrogated him to the point where he told you everything. Then measures had to be made." He finishes talking with a smirk.

"You did that? What do you mean 'interrogated'? I didn't do shit; he gave up that information on his own. He was proud to do it."

Blood laughs, "Heh, may he then spend eternity with the Poderoso Dios he prayed over."

I make a frown, "you killed your man for nothing. Plus, how did you kill your own man?"

"Some advice mi hijo, you want the omelet you must break the-."

Interrupting the middle of another 'more you know' moment with Blood is an explosion originating in the hallways behind us. It was loud enough to shake everything including the contents in my head.

With Blood facing the area where the noise is coming from he gets a better view than I do. The look on his painted up face is one of anger and confusion. He starts to growl. I try very hard not to laugh.

Someone pops out from behind me to say, "Maestro, we are being attacked, they found us."

Blood immediately looks at me as I am still laying on my knees. With fiery fury beaming from his eyes he screams one word while pointing in my direction, "you!"

I turn around to make sure he's not talking to someone else laying on their knees directly behind me. I turn back with the most dumbfounded look on my face, "what-."

Just then the large glass part of the roof smashes. I had never noticed this part of the ceiling before because they had spray painted it black.

Pieces of glass start to rain on our heads. I cover myself since my arms weren't tied together this time. Blood on the other hand is more concerned with who's attacking him than his own well-being.

Ropes descend from the ceiling down to the ground. As men dressed head to toe in black make their way down the ropes, Blood turns his attention back on me.

"You," he starts yelling again as he points. "You did this! You brought them here! Gusanito!" He then rips off his suit jacket and dress shirt with tie and lets out a blood curdling scream, "Aarrgghh!!!"

Before he can come at me the men dangling from high above have landed. They start attacking Blood. He answers with grabbing two of them by their faces. He looks at me and says, "You remember puta, you made me do this," as I hear the cracking and crushing of bones. I look on shocked yet surprisingly unremorseful.

As he disregards the bodies nonchalantly and with ease, I start to think that maybe I should go. I start to stand up. I'm having trouble however since I've been on my knees and it turns out my legs are stiff. Not that I noticed before trying to escape.

Finally, I get on my feet and head for the door. Blood's screaming followed by the sound of more bone crushing echo inside my ears. Finding the exit is harder than I had planned. It's very dark and I have no idea how to get through this maze.

Eventually I start to see a speck of light which leads me to the cool breeze of freedom. Outside there are bodies lying around parked cars. I look around I notice I walked out of a warehouse surrounded by a junkyard.

Quickly it dawns on me that I know where I am, in an industrial part of the city. There's a bus nearby. I go through the front gate which looks like it had been blown open.

I eventually make it back to my building with the recent events still ringing in my head. Walking up the stairs I start to long for some sweet hutch and some beauty sleep. Well, more like a coma than a sleep.

That all gets flushed away when I arrived at my front door. The smell of cinnamon starts seeping out of the office from under the door. It fills the hallway joining the already faint scent.

Opening it by the doorway stands the linchpin to this madness. The start and hopefully end of all of this. Maria, in all her glory looking pretty as a depressing picture. Her look almost exact as the first time I met her. The exact day and time of that moment, I have no idea. You could argue that finding the body was the start to all this. It really wasn't any more than just something to forget about until she, lack of a better phrase, walked into my life.

I walk past her and head to the desk looking inside for a hidden bottle of hutch. No dice.

Again it's Deja vu all over again as she stands there crying in her hand. Once again wearing that low crop top to show off her goods. She apologizes for the way she ran off last time. With her head down she extends her hand out filled with crumbled money.

She says "you must end the Diablo. He no get away from murdering my sweet poor Jesús."

"Yeah," I answer as I scratch my head. Not only out of awkwardness, but out of confusion. "I'm not going to do that."

She's crying, puts her arm down. She falls down on her knees, drops the money and is literally begging me to kill Blood.

This almost touches my heart. Almost, if I wasn't so tired and thirsty. Also, I'm still a little untrustworthy of her. I walk over and am about to grab her by the arms to life her up. Before I do, I look down her top. I didn't mean to, it was a moment of lapse judgment, I don't believe that either.

As I'm looking down, feeling like a real jerk for once this whole time, I notice another tattoo. It's also lighten by makeup just like the one on her right shoulder.

This one is on her left breast just above her heart. Unlike her other tat this one isn't as lighten. Before I decipher the image in my head I wonder why I didn't notice it before. Perhaps the makeup or maybe I really wasn't looking. Expecting another gang tattoo I realize it's a star. A shaded in star like a black star or a dark star.

'Fuck' I scream at myself in my head. Here I was just starting to feel bad for her. In my own way. I have to play this smart. I take a step back. While still on her knees as she's waiting for me to help her up I say, "We missed you earlier Darkstar."

My comment has caused silence. Just like a faucet that was her tear ducts they've been shut off abruptly.

She stands up, slowly. Her body in the standing position is so straight, straighter than I've ever seen her. She raises her head slowly. No more tears, no more sniveling, her eyes pierce mine. "How long," she utters two words.

"For a while now." I lie, terribly.

"You are a terrible liar." She notices and her accent has melted away. "If only you were as good as a fibber as you are a detective. I have misjudged you."

Everything becomes clear. "There is no Jesús. At least he's not your brother. I doubt that's even his real name. I'm sure you're not Maria either. Those names were so common. You knew I was never going to find you in the system. Not taking his body that made me suspicious."

"Then, magically, he disappeared. You're doing I'm sure. Was he one of your Fearless Five?"

She was impressed by my knowledge. "It really was my mistake to misjudge you."

"You made more than one. You were a part of Blood's crew. You didn't want me to find that out. That's why you tried to hide your gang tattoo. You then left him to start your own crew.

You wanted to begin a war, but something got in the way."

"My guess would be, Jesús. Poor Jesús got in the way. So you faked an O.D., that kid wasn't an addict. He had never shot up before. Plus, he was right handed. No way would he have done that with his left. You fucked up big time on that one, probably was in a rush." Take that Jessica Fletcher!

She puts her head down, she's smiling, "you done?"

I squint. "I don't know; you tell me?"

She bends down and pulls something out of her knee high boots. Did I forget about that? Oh yeah, fuck me boots, and tight ass pants. Painted on pants as she tried to distract me with sex. Classic distraction technique.

She pulls out a butterfly knife out of one of the boots. She flicks her wrist and exposes the blade. "I might as tell you everything. Seeing has how you're going to die very soon."

What is this shit? It's the villain exposition, a goddamn monologue! Here I thought Blood was dramatic. She holds the knife to her side. Am I hanging above a vat of sharks or some shit? I hate this clichéd shit!

"The name I was given when I joined Blood's crew was D-Nice. Blood was building an empire and I wanted on the ground floor so to speak. While the high rise was being constructed I quickly realized I wasn't expected to be just another soldier."

"Blood wanted all the few women that were in the crew to be nothing more than concubines. To be used as an incentive or encouragement to the crew. He took for himself as well."

"You hear about the plight of the working woman. This isn't much different. No man is going to follow a woman in this business." Business is she serious? A regular Susan B. Anthony this one.

"Of course I refused, but not without resistance. I managed to have enough time before I would be forced into being a sex slave. I had to gather some forces. Blood manages to manipulate his soldiers and upper management into making them his 'followers'."

"I was able to achieve what I thought was the impossible. I found four other members who hadn't been sucked into Blood's 'cult'. One of them was young Jesús. You are right in the knowledge that wasn't his real name." No fucking duh.

"We broke off from the crew. I named us the 'Fearless Five'. I wanted to continue the dramatics that had begun with Blood. I knew that was the only way he would listen." Bullshit, you keep telling yourself that. You got caught with the actor's bug.

"I was reborn as Darkstar. The only way I could gain respect and be heard was to stay in the shadows. I knew everyone would assume I was a man."

"We started recruiting as we tried to make as much trouble for Blood as we could. We started off as five but grew into twenty. With my dedicated group I knew we needed to do something to cement ourselves as true threats. We needed to blow up Blood's warehouse. He is planning something and it started with that place."

My shoulders shrug up. "Is there an intermission at this show?" My question causes her to walk closer to me with the knife pointed out. "Ok I get it calm down. Can I sit at least?" She nods and I take a deserved sit. She tilts her head back and continues.

"We went in and we were good. We were silent, they never knew we were coming. The one thing we didn't plan on, was there not being any drugs. We killed the guards, took out the cameras, it was orchestrated beautifully. I was prouder than a parent with my little army."

"It wasn't until the charges were set that we found out Blood had an army of young recruits housed in there. He was training them to be his 'death squad'. It was too late. The fuse was lit and it was like fucking Christmas. We lit up the sky, kind of a turn on."

"Afterwards Jesús found out his cousin was in there. I can't say it didn't bother me a little. Nonetheless, what's a few eggs you know?"

I interrupt her. "You sound like Blood," she didn't like hearing that. "You mean to tell me you blew up that place without really knowing what was in there? You did all that research prior but just gave up? After what, you casually looked under the couch? People fucking died, horribly!"

She starts to look embarrassed. "We didn't know there was a trap door! They weren't innocent, they were still the enemy!" She starts to get angry, "I'll fucking stab you!"

I yell back, "no you won't! You need an audience, Dame Judi Dench! Whatever, I don't care anymore, keep going Hamlet!"

She composes herself. "Little chocha, don't really know if it was fear or his own guilt but he ratted us out to Blood. He had been feeding him our whereabouts. What we had been planning. We started to get a footing on the drug supply. We became more than a whisper. Graduated from being an urban legend, especially after the fire."

"He had to fuck it up. With the help of the rest of the original five we trapped him on that roof. He didn't touch drugs; he was a good soldier that way. Giving him a speedball I knew he would O.D. being his first shot with that recipe. The pigs would never care about a dumb junkie. They usually don't here."

"I had planned on playing the sister and just blame it on Blood. Then you happened to be there. The drunk knight in shitty armor. I saw you on TV. To be honest, you looked like a fool. A stupid drunk gringo. I could smell the fumes off the TV. Lo and behold, you're a fucking detective. It turned out to be my luck."

"You provided the address. I came over showed some tears and shook my tits. How ironic, the very things that stopped me from advancing in my gang. They were my very two 'assets' that got you to notice." Being on TV is turning out to be more trouble than it was worth.

I was in the middle of making the hand gesture to let's speed this along. When her offensive words hit my ears. I stopped her. "Wait a fucking minute, I resent that! Your little sex game didn't work. The only asset you had that turned me on was that paper. You underestimated me."

She reluctantly says "I did. The idea became to make you the patsy.

Who would believe the smelly drunkard?" Touché. "It would have been easy to frame you. Then get rid of you. You just had to sniff around."

Unfortunately, she keeps going. "I needed information first, to know how much Blood knew. The last time I saw you I learned he caught on to you fast."

"I had to get away. Couldn't let him know I was the one who had hired you. This happened before I could get any real info from you. That's it, you're now all caught up. Now you are going to bring me the head of Hermano de Sangre."

When she finishes my eyes snap open. "What, oh, you're done? I was dozing off. I had this unwanted guest in my office. They told this story that kept going and had no end to it. Oh, you're still here." I get up from the couch and stretch. "How, pray tell, is this going to happen? Please, no drawn out plans."

She ignores me. "What did Blood tell you?"

"He thought I was a part of your crew and he wanted me to bring you to him." I yawn.

"Of course he did. Fucking idiota. So you are going to do just that. He's gonna get a surprise out of it too."

She starts to walk closer to me. "Before we go along with your brilliant plan, you have to answer some questions. It's my OCD. A need to know everything or else my head will explode."

She sighs, "Fine, what is it"?

"Hey, I listened to your bullshit!" I take a deep breath. "Ok, first, what the hell happened to Blood's henchman the one I was talking to? Actually that's it." I smile devilishly.

"Hermano de Sangre is extremely paranoid. Everyone in The Dead has a chip placed in the back of their neck under the skin. Located below the skull, but above the spine."

"This chip when activated creates an ignition that then creates a small combustion. It goes throughout your nervous system. Ultimately, it melts your face. Turns everything around you into scolding ash. It's like having napalm coming out of every orifice."

"The death chips are controlled by remote controls. Blood has all of them. He lets his captains secure some of them. That's who you saw driving off on the cycle."

I hate this Bond shit. "That's some ridiculous NASA like tech. Where would Bloody get that shit from? It wouldn't be coming from the puppet master would it"? Turns out I had more questions.

She seems surprised that I'm aware of that info, "I don't know his name. That is just a nickname Blood gave him. I don't think he wants anyone to know who he is. It's possible."

"You said he's paranoid that would explain why he had someone following the guy who followed me.

You're lucky none of them saw and recognized you. What about earlier today? With Blood's lair?"

She smiles as she talks about it. "That was another well-orchestrated plan. I had you followed when you got picked up. As you commented before I was not there. A leader doesn't always need to lead on the battlefield. That's what makes a good leader, to be able to send the troops out and not have to worry about them losing."

"You blew up yet another warehouse. This time it didn't have a bunch of defenseless people stuck in the basement. No, it just had one giant who might be mentally challenged. Congratulations on your exploits. By the way, I don't think I would consider that a win either, he did kill some of your guys."

"Did we not kill more of his?"

Frustrated I say, "I'm done, talking to you deranged fucks hurts my brain. Alright, let's go, after you."

She insists I go first and she walks behind me. I can feel the pressure the knife makes on my back. We head outside. Diagonally across the street I see the guy on the motorcycle from before. He's just staring at us still has his helmet on. We walk closer to where he is in the street without crossing it.

Next to my building is an alleyway. It's one of those double wide ones. With giant garbage metal storage bins. As we pass the dark, smelly alley our attention is still to the henchman on the bike.

From the darkness comes a voice, "from within the shadows the spider emerges to devour the fly." We both turn around quickly with are heads buzzing. There stands Hermano de Sangre in all his painted up goodness. Standing in front of a small army of men. The look on my face is one of monotony.

Her face seems to be painted with fear. Almost going pale white in seconds. "Well little fly, those grains of sand in your hourglass are dwindling down. Are you ready to be devoured?" He says in his deep loud voice with a smirk. He doesn't seem too surprised that Darkstar is a woman.

He then turns his attention to me. "And you, gusano blanco, you run off from a battle like a little girl. Did you shit yourself again? Hermano de Sangre has determined that you do not work for Darkstar."

"Oh really," I reply. "How did you figure that one out I wonder? Maybe it's the fucking knife sticking in my back? You should give up your life being a WWE heel and become a Marlowe. Idiot."

Like usual everyone ignores me.

The color starts to return in D's face. As soon as she starts to hear engines that drive up behind us. They belong to her army. She starts to talk with a smirk on her face. "You're not the only one who has their followers being followed. Get ready for some

Indigestion." This is being said like we're in a Schwarzenegger movie. With a straight face. Just terrible.

Here I am now in the middle of this gang war. This recreation of West Side Story. Fists are flying, knives are slicing skin exposing blood, and someone pulled out a gun. I'm getting the fuck out of here.

There are more important things in life. Like me and maybe puppies. I know how to take care of myself but I can't dodge bullets. I keep ducking while trying to get out of this alleyway. Someone just flew right past me.

Finally, out of the melee. Before I turn the corner I look and see the small frame of D-Nice and the large wrestler like frame of that painted face jackass Hermano de Sangre. They're both staring at each other, breathing heavy. His make-up is messed up a little from all the head-butting he's been doing and the girl has blood on her.

"You are going to wish you had become Hermano de Sangre's woman." Can be heard being said by the jackass with the bigger God complex. It makes me feel so warm inside when he speaks in the third person. Oh wait, I meant sick.

I would care about all this, but I'm tired. This thing has been draining and plus there's no reward in watching. What, more blood? No thanks. Besides, as I'm walking up to my office I notice I've got some red spots on me from the OK corral down there. Have to remember to burn this shirt.

I get in my office and I can still hear the fight from my window. I sit down on the couch. I release a big exhale now trying to forget all this drama. I turn my ugly head for the only thing my liver craves, hutch.

I am disappointed to realize I have nothing to drink. I must get some tomorrow. My eyelids get heavy. The sounds of bloodshed just a few feet from my ears must be soothing to me.

I reflect on everything that's happened. My eyes close. The swollen one has gotten better to the point where I can open and close it. My arm is better; lips are less swollen. I haven't been beaten up in a while. Still got some money. There are the bills still on my floor from before.

Turned out being not a terrible end. Sacrificing the blackouts to just being tired better be worth it. Hope I don't regret this and have any nightmares. I think about how I wouldn't want to do any of it over again though. As for everything that happened outside, ugh, let's say the girl, D-Nice? Yeah, she died.

PART II: MY HEART FLOATS ON

THE BOTTOM OF THE BOTTLE

1

Once again we find our 'hero' during his favorite pastime, drinking. Sitting in a dank bar alone and chugging poison in one's body may not be your idea of a good time. For Champ however, he's never been in a happier, calmer mood.

Unfortunately, good fortune never lasts when it comes to him. Without his misery the world would be a boring place to live. Reintroducing the man without a conscience, Champ.

I'm content. I want to smile. I haven't been touched lately. All the lacerations, bumps, and bruises on my body have mostly healed. Leaving behind scars and creating stories and memories that will last forever.

Got some money in my shoes. From giving blood and donating my body to science, that sort of thing. I really want to smile. I don't though, I don't want people to notice me. They might get the wrong impression. Besides if I do, I'll be advertising my good fortune. Someone will want the benefits or bring me down.

So I sulk over my hutch and smirk. Just then the bartender comes over. "What are you smiling about hunched over? You look nefarious."

"Big word for a high school dropout." I'm only assuming. I swallow the rest of my hutch. "Why don't you get me another of whatever I'm consuming Sam?"

His brow gets wrinkled, "for the last time that's not my name." He walks away in a huff.

"Wait, I'm not in Cheers? Oh right, the pools of vomit on the floor should have tipped me off." I point at the poor excuse of the waitress. "I thought Carla looked hairier than usual."

He comes back with my hutch. "Here, don't choke."

I go to take a swig, "did you spit in this?" He doesn't look back as he walks away. "Ah, it's ok." I say as I swipe my hand in the air and go to put the cup to my lips, "I've drank worse." It's true, sometimes it's been liquids you use to strip paint off of things. Occasionally it'll be liquids to help disinfect your hands.

I'm so happy with myself, it's nauseating. A small part in my brain is gnawing at me. It's telling me this will not last. I ignore it and try to drown it. This watering hole is not a regular haunt for me. Honestly, I don't care for this place.

It's a bit of a shithole. Not the kind of shithole I like. I enjoy attempts at trying to be hip, trying to be different. This place is just a shithole purely on not giving a shit. It is however one of the few places in my neighborhood that hasn't barred me. Who knew hutch was flammable even when you put it in the toilet? So did I.

I look at the bartender whose back is to me. "Hey, you got any nuts, popcorn, or pretzels? I want something to nibble on."

"You're gonna get my fist to nibble on in a minute if you don't shut up." He mutters to himself, but I hear him.

I start to laugh. "That's cool man, I hate you too. You know you should really-"Just then I feel a tug from behind me. I turn my stool around, "huh?"

It's a little girl, blond hair, big eyes, and a sad look on her face. "Mister, I need your help."

I'm confused but I turn my stool back to the bar. "Sam, am I that drunk or is there a kid in the bar?"

She tugs at me again. "Please mister, I really need your help." She says as I hear the bartender screaming something about his name. It's hard trying to ignore two annoying things at once. She extends her arm, clenching something in her hand, "please just look."

She put it in my lap, it's a piece of paper. I open it and there's a picture of a dog. A scrappy looking one. The kind that Annie used to have, Sandy. Under the picture is a phone number. Above the picture in bold letters is, LOST.

I turn to the kid, "you want me to find your puppy?"

She starts to get excited. "Yes please, I miss Piddles so much!"

I make a scrunchy look on my face, "Piddles, oh now I'm definitely not doing it."

She gets upset, "please mister." Then she says something that I'm sure she thinks she's clever for saying.

"Come on mister, could you really say no to a cute little guy-"

"Yes, yes I can." I cut her off. I knew where she was going. You can't tug at heartstrings that are too stretched out from previous abuse. "The answer is still no."

She put her head down and walks out of the bar. Honestly, a little girl thinks she can get me to help her find her dog? I've done some crap jobs, but this would take the proverbial cake.

I leave the bar. I get to my humble abode. I walk up to the second floor. I'm drunk, very drunk. I'm close to getting to the blackouts, but I'm clear enough to still function.

I open the door to my office. I'm ready to continue my party until the liquor god, Distillo takes me to

Blackout Land. I'm closing my front door as I remark to myself how clever I am.

My self-admiration gets disrupted by a hand that goes straight to my throat. "If it isn't the upstanding citizen of the year." It's my attentive Landlord, Derek Powers. He's a lot like Mr. Roper but instead of being a homophobe, he's just a sociopath.

He's got me up against the frame of my front door. A little more to the left and I would had broken glass. His grip on me is tight. Pain, no, but it's getting harder to breathe. "What do you want? I'm paid up." My voice sounds raspy, takes me a second to realize why.

"I just came by for a friendly visit. Isn't that what landlord's do?" He chuckles.

He's drunk, not as drunk as I am. His inhibitions are a lot looser than mine though. I'm about to get to the blackouts like I wanted. Just not how I wanted. "Oh, is that all? Sure, let go of my throat and I'll make you some tea." It's getting harder to make quips.

He laughs, "always with the jokes. Maybe not for much longer I'm thinking."

His grip gets tighter. What does Captain Thunder say in this situation? Move #66, 'When in need, go for the eyes.'

Good idea. I'm about to use what's left of my strength to raise my hands, thumbs extended. That's when he comes closer to my face with his shit eating grin. "But why end it? Power is not found in guns, fists, or even money. It's information that topples governments. Its secrets that keep people in line."

He gets real close to my left ear. He starts to whisper in it like we're on the playground and he's going to say he has a crush on me. "Isn't that right, mister...?"

That's when he does it. That's when he says those two words that stop me from lunging my thumbs into his eyes and into the back of his skull. Those two words that sunk into my chest and took out my heart. Those two words that can do what no one can normally do, make me speechless.

He lets me go and I fall to my knees. With the shocked and confusing look he put on my face he leaves. His laughing echoes down the halls and to the foyer of the building, like a banshee at the moon. I'm left there on my knees. At a loss of words, of actions. The hole he left in me must be filled with the only cement I would ever want.

I finish the last of my bottles in my special reserve. I start to get to the blackouts. As light is traded with darkness, my last thought is of Powers. Those two words he said to me took whatever happiness I had within me. How the hell did he know my real name?

2

I open my eyes slowly. Takes a second to recollect the moments of yesterday. I get up to look for a bottle so I could bleach out those memories.

My throat sounds sore as I blow out some air in disappointment.

I now have to take this problem head on. With no liquid courage in sight no less. Fine, as much as I hate dealing with reality, let's do it. How does he know my name? Why does he know it?

When I first rented out this office it was owned by an old man. The neighborhood had been gradually getting better. This was one of the last buildings that hadn't been bought up and gentrified. He had no intention to sell. Didn't charge me much in the way of rent either and he was laid back when I didn't pay on time.

Of course I took full advantage of that. There was also no lease. I never knew why because I didn't care. I think it was because he was just nice and didn't want to create any hassle.

Then crime rose drastically higher within the next few years. That was around the time Powers acquired the building. He was aggressive from the start. Always demanded the rent with his fists. The somewhat 'decent' tenants got replaced with drug dealers. Once again never talk of a lease.

I had always thought it was for a shadier reason. That's why I wasn't worried about Powers discovering my full name. I never thought much about what happened to that old man since I was too distracted, makes me wonder now.

I usually don't get hungover, but my head hurts. Feels like an ax wedged in my brain. Almost wish there really was one. I can't do this. The brain quakes I'm experiencing is stopping me from zoning. The best way to cure this is to spend the rest of my money on hutch.

I nerve up enough energy to put on new clothes. I open my front door to get wasted for the morning. This is a good idea.

I get into my hallway. By the stairs, sleeping on the floor is the little girl from the bar. I squat down to wake her up. "Hey, little lady, gotta wake up. Are you that desperate that you've been sleeping here all morning?"

She gives me a wtf look. "All morning? It's 3 in the afternoon. I just got here two hours ago. I even knocked on the door, you didn't answer. Wow, you must be a heavy sleeper mister."

"Yeah, that's it." I say in a raspy voice as I roll my eyes a little.

She shakes her head. "Anyway, you gonna take my case now?"

Aw, she's so cute, like I'd give a crap about her life. "No darling, because you don't have a 'case'." I talk as I walk down the stairs and onto the sidewalk. She follows. "What you have is something that would be more suitable for Encyclopedia Brown."

The sun cracks out through the cloud patterns to pierce my eyes and start a fire in my brain. Which it seems to do often. This only aggravates my headache.

"Should I try him, where does he live?" She asks.

I rub my well-deserved dry eyes. "No Hun, he's not, nevermind. Look, I'd love to but I don't do Pro Bono."

"Oh ok, I don't know what that is." Her big sad eyes fail to land on mine.

"Come on kid, cash, cheese, Mr. Greenjeans. Money hunny and you ain't got none." Trapping this kid is giving me unashamed joy.

I walk down the streets with my destination set. I could just get hutch from the corner. I like ambiance instead, and being able to piss off the booze jockeys. Heidi is still behind me. "Oh No mister, I have money."

Shit, I was hoping she wouldn't have any. Me love money. On the other hand, I'm not at desperate times just yet. What's a little girl doing walking around this shit hole carrying cash? When I find her rockface parents I'm gonna slap them in the food hole.

I turn around to face her. "Look, a five pounder won't cut it. Now stop following me. I'm saying this nicely. You can't cross the street without holding an adult's hand. Since I don't see an adult anywhere, have to stay here. Tootles cutiepie."

I start crossing the street as she says, "but, but, but mister, wait." Her voice fades as I get closer to my stop, the Reagle Beagle. It's based on the bar from the sitcom Three's Company. It's meant to induce nostalgia. All it really provided was a nasty lawsuit.

Inside the soon to be closing bar I'm sitting holding my drink reflecting on that little girl. I don't feel bad for her. It's just, I really don't feel bad for her. That exchange did help me forget about last night. So there was one good thing about it.

This place has gone downhill since its fate was announced to be sealed. The owners gave up caring so a lot of the décor has been stolen. None of the toilets in this time machine longer work. Too lazy to try the women's room so I pee in the sink.

I don't care about the look of the place. I care that they still have hutch, if barely. I care about getting hutch faced. I care about the blackouts.

Later that night, say last call later, I'm still at the bar. I got the doubles. I'm ready for blast off. I'm like a Metallica song. I'm about to fade to black.

3

My eyes feel as heavy as two garage doors. My brain sends the impulse to my eyes to try to open them. After many repeated attempts they finally start to open albeit slowly.

My memory has become Swiss cheese. I seem to be in my office. I just don't remember how I got here. My enemy the sun is getting through my blinds. Their usually closed. Someone is sitting in my chair at the desk. I can't make out who.

"Do you have solitaire on this computer mister? Is this like the first computer ever made?" It's her, Shirley Temple. She has become my living tumor.

"How?" The lack of power in my brain causes me to speak in fragments. The next word is going to take a while to form.

"You fell out of the bar. You couldn't stand up. You couldn't speak. I was so afraid. I thought you were going to die. Then you would never find my Piddles," she says.

The next word comes out like a ticker tape. "Late." What the hell was she doing out so late? Next one comes, "Parents." Where the hell were her parents? I wish my speaking words were as expressive.

"It's ok mister. Mr. Black helped you into the car. We drove you here. I slept in the car, I came up here a few hours ago." She says, I take in the words drunkenly confused.

As I've said before I rarely get hungover. This apparently is another one of those 'rare' occasions. My brain is a heavy brick on fire and I am very dehydrated.

Water is something I try to avoid. There are things in our reservoir that should not be consumed by humans. Right now I am desperate, I need it bad. I try to look at my sink, "Water."

"This computer should be in a museum mister." She doesn't pay attention.

I get up like an old man with arthritis in everything. I hobble over to the sink in the bathroom. I cup my hands and lap the crap that came out of my faucet. Throat becomes less dry. That occasional fire in my brain starts to go out.

When I speak I sound less raspy too. "Ok, fill me in. What car, who's Mr. Black, and where are the rents?"

She takes me outside. Parked in front of my building is a black sedan. Inside is a man in a black suit. Blond guy, Mr. Black. He could be her father they look so similar, turns out he isn't.

He gets out of the car. He comes to the curb and doesn't say anything. Just stands there with his hands behind him. Little girl speaks, "Mr. Black is the driver."

I go from looking down at her to looking up at him, he's tall. "That is correct," is all he says.

I look back down at her while in the middle of this odd uneven sandwich. "Who's your father, hun?"

She answers, "My father, well, he's my daddy."

I look back up at the driver. He speaks, "Mr. Herodes."

I answer back with a question with my eyes squinted, "Atticus Herodes?"

Black responses with just a slight nod.

Atticus Herodes is a philanthropist. He just built a new pediatric wing at the hospital. Not the one I go to but a good one.

He made his money on stocks. Didn't really start making a name for himself until he got into the real estate game. Hey, I know some things, I read about him in a newspaper. It was framed in front of a urinal.

It's been said he has a good heart. That he's one of the 'good ones'.

Compared to what? I don't believe in that pure of heart crap. Everyone's got grey in them. There's degrees in this sort of thing. You see me, my heart looks like a dog just took a steamy crap. Put me next to Joel Rifkin murderer of nine prostitutes and I look like Prince Charming with a B.O. problem.

I look back down at the girl. "Where is your daddy hun?"

Mr. Black answers me instead, quietly. "He's been missing for three days. She's been informed. She seems more concerned with her dog." Maybe she's in denial or shock.

Wonderful, this is getting me closer to real money though. Maybe I can squeeze my way into finding the Monopoly man instead of the mutt. My indifference starts to creep into my head full of pain. Now a part of me just wants to relax and get hutch faced.

I feel a tug on my arm. "I tried to tell you yesterday mister. I didn't have five dollars. I just took the largest number there was." She says holding a Franklin.

"I'll find your dog." I answer quickly.

She gets ecstatic. "Oh thank you, thank you mister!"

Arms wrap around my legs as she begins hugging them. "Ok, ok enough. Where was he last seen?"

Mr. Black tells me Herodes went to the local park to take the dog for a walk. That was the last either of them were seen. Guess that's my first stop.

She hands me the money. Putting it away in my shoe I notice I didn't spend all my money last night. Things are definitely starting to turn up. "Ok mister, give me your cell number so you can text me when you get any information." She pulls out a cellphone that looks more expensive than my entire wardrobe.

"Yeah, I don't really have one." I say not at all ashamed that this little girl is more advanced than me. "How old are you anyway, six?"

"I'm eight." She answers sharply.

I frown my brow. "Oh, still aren't you too young to have one?"

"Aren't you too old not to have one?" Touché, I'm starting to like this kid.

"Out of curiosity, how did you find me?" I ask ignoring her zing.

"We saw you on the T.V.!" She answers excitedly. "Mr. Black and I were watching my favorite show in the whole world, That Generic Non-Threatening Sitcom Show, when the news came on. I don't like the news." She finishes with a sad look on her face.

I remark to myself that they're not even trying with these crappy titles anymore when Black starts to clarify. "The news came on immediately following the show. You were being interviewed about an unfortunate accident involving that young man."

"Accident," I interrupt him with my not really Tourette's acting up. "That kid fell to his deat-" Before I can finish Black reminds me of my insensitivity in front of the kid by slowly and calmly shaking his head.

He continues, "We quickly turned off the TV but not before remarking on your appearance."

"I said you looked smelly." She says unapologetically. If this kid is trying to get into my good graces, it's working.

"When this, unfortunate situation arose, she remembered seeing you on the news due to her good memory. It took time to track you down."

"Wow that was a convenient explanation."

Soon after they drive off. Putting the missing poster of the dog in my pocket I realize I do not know the name of the little girl. Plus, they could have given me a ride to that park.

After drinking for a few hours, you know, so I could break that hunny the little girl gave me. I reluctantly had to call a cab for this one. The poor man's chariot does not go to the rich neighborhoods. Problem is I don't know where Atticus Herodes lives.

I call one of the local papers from the bar to try to get an idea of what neighborhood he lives in.

Imagine that, a guy from the paper answering a call with rowdy people and Motley Crue in the background. Along with some creepy guy asking you where the richest man in the city lives. Not the address just the area as if that makes it better. No surprise the guy hung up on me.

I'm waiting for the cab as I start to think where he could live. There aren't too many what you would call 'good neighborhoods' for white's who have money.

A best hypothetical guess would be the gated community of Kalani. It's up in the hills. It's not the only rich area. It is the newest one, so it's worth a shot at being the first. When the car comes I tell the driver.

We get to the beautiful secluded community surrounded by a forest up in the hills known as, Kalani. It's so far up and away from the crud of the city. I believe the Mayor lives in here. Makes sense to be far away from your constituents when they hate you so much they want to kill you.

Before getting into the posh community we stop at the entrance. There's a problem, the guards at the main gate won't let me in. I mention having an appointment with Atticus Herodes. I throw Mr. Black's name. They both equal a big nothing. I think about saying 'I'm here for a little girl.' Then I decide that's not a good idea.

The car leaves me down the hill from the main gate. I start zoning about how to get in. There could be a back door. It might be smaller, easier to get into.

I don't have the time to walk around this place. It's gotta be huge. I realize I'm standing on the side of a highway in my zone pose. I must look like a psycho to the cars that zoom by. If I had a dollar for every time I looked like a psycho I wouldn't need to look for a lost puppy.

I continue to stand there contemplating on how I'm going to get in. I can't help but drift my thoughts to why I think this Herodes guy is full of shit. You live here yet you claim to be a 'man of the people'? Everyone's full of it eventually.

People are like onions, they smell, are layered, are good in a stew, and when you get to their core are full of shit. Ok, maybe not completely like onions.

I play at the scenario of walking around this massive compound. In my head I am going through the forest, walking over rocks and tree stumps carefully making sure I don't hurt myself.

Then finding the wall that surrounds all the houses so I can find the perfect spot. Some sort of chink, real word, a flaw that I can take advantage of.

Then I get the better idea of walking back up the hill. To use my world class charm to get them to let me in. If that doesn't work and let's face it, it won't, there's always the lump in my shoe.

I go back to the security checkpoint at the main gate. Inside is a fat older man, with white hair who looks like the skipper. Let's hope he's as cuddly as he looks.

He's reading a newspaper and ignoring my existence as I stand for a minute. Why do I feel like I've been down this road before? After getting him to finally look up at me he tells me

I'm not allowed in. Not without a pass from a resident or an appointment.

"No I know that already I just came up here with a taxi a few minutes ago. I just thought I could offer you some kind of proposition?" I'm definitely better at this than climbing a fucking wall. I try to avoid the physical stuff anyway. I'd rather not waste my money or something that is not hutch. It trumps climbing a wall though.

The guard perks up at my idea. His mouth turns into a smirk and both eyebrows start to raise. "You mean sex," he asks excitedly.

"What? No!" I respond horrified. "I was talking about money."

"Oh", he sounded disappointed. "How much you offering?"

"Five dollars," I say while smiling.

Turns out he wanted more than that. I had to shell out fifty bucks. He wasn't cuddly like the skipper at all. I asked for a ride, which would cost me another twenty-five. This is my life, one minute I'm on cloud nine, the next, I'm down seventy-five dollars. I'm just lucky I had a little money left over before I got that hunny.

As he drops me off by the park he says "don't rape anyone." Best security money can buy.

I walk in the small gated playground. The park is centered with houses surrounding the area. How am I going to find what it is I don't know I'm looking for? It's just starting to get dark too. Clues, clues, looking for clues. There's a lot of trees in this park.

Maybe if I start with the entrance. I'm lucky there are no kids here.

One of the first trees you come to when entering the park has a dog turd near it. I'll bet this little deuce belongs to the kid's mutt. Besides tasting the thing and bringing it to a lab, how would I know?

Maybe the bit of blood that's on some of the leaves at the bottom of the tree helps my guess. I'm thinking this belongs to poppa. Maybe the dog ran off? Why wouldn't the cops collect this, didn't they see it?

This has been a long day. My body needs a rest, and some hutch. I don't think that's going to happen anytime soon though.

Gotta get myself out of here. Out of the front gate from which I came.

Then hitchhiking here I come. Maybe the skipper will give me a ride. If I had the money. Or if I gave him something else. I'm not that desperate. It's been a long day, gonna be a long night-

"Mister, hey mister!" That voice is one decibel away from being a shrill. I know that almost shrill. It's the little girl running to me by the entrance of the park. I walk away from the bloody tree towards her.

"What are you doing here?" I ask her as she comes up to me.

"I live a block away. I'm out looking for Piddles." She says with missing posters in her hand.

"What about your mom? Where's Mr. Black?"

"Mommy died of the grown up sickness." She's says with her head down.

I start to see Black come out of the darkness. "Hey, you know the least you could have done was driven me here Blacky." I say pissed pointing at him. He just stares. "You think the least you could do is drive me home?" He turns his head to look at the little girl.

"Did you find anything on Piddles, mister?"

"Not really darling." I just lied to a child. I won't lose sleep over it.

"Oh no!" She starts to cry. She runs to Black. He puts his arm around her.

"So how about that ride?" I say, ignoring the crying kid.

Black shakes his head.

"Why the hell not!?!" I yell as he's still holding the kid.

"Don't like you." He says short and sweet.

"Oh, well ok, I understand that." I give up quickly. I'm still pissed but I wouldn't give me a ride either. As they turn to walk away, I watch them. They walk another block, take a left turn then disappear.

I guess I'm on my own again. Maybe this gives me the opportunity to check some blocks. Walking around this neighborhood has to be done quietly. Once people see me it's going to raise some flags. So no saying to people 'a little girl asked me to come here', as was my original plan. I'm starting to realize why people think I'm creepy.

I'm finding it difficult to keep a low profile on this one. There are no sidewalks, I'm walking on the side of the road here. If that just doesn't scream 'I look like the kind of guy who has to tell you I'm moving into the neighborhood by law'.

If the dog ran off he couldn't be too far. It's dark now. Looking through people's driveways isn't the best plan. This doesn't seem to work. I'm feeling defeated and I've got a long way home. I have to find my way back to the front gate.

Maybe climbing a wall isn't such a bad idea right now. Going against my better judgement. I start going through the trees between two houses. To my right between the trees I can see the side of the other house in the distance. I'm not paying attention until I hear the crash of a garbage can.

I turn my head. Squinting my eyes from the light on the side of the house I can see the cans. I see an animal going through them. Pulling out something from the garbage is a dog. I pull out the missing poster. I think it's the fucking mutt!

I run over dodging trees and rocks careless of me but fuck it. As I get closer I recognize it as the leash is still on the little turd. He notices me but gets spooked in the process. He starts to growl.

"Easy boy, I'm just trying to help." As I get closer I notice red spots on him. I try to grab him; he bites me on my left hand barely breaking the skin. "Motherfucker."

I go to grab him again, this time faster. I got him. He's not too heavy, a medium size dog but a little scrawny. I look closely at the red, its dry blood. He keeps snipping at me. I look at his collar. It looks tight on him. The collar part on the top of his neck is protruding a bit. Something of a bump.

There's something wedged between the collar and his neck. I push it out. Little thing squeals a bit. Must have been hurting him a lot. The dog starts to lick my face. Little shithead just bit me, now I'm his hero. My reward is dog drool.

I open my hand to look at my prize. It's a cassette tape. One of those mini ones that come with voice recorders. I think I got a lead.

I walk the dog back to the little girl's block. I'm starting to think I won't be able to find the house. When I get there I notice a huge house bigger than any of the houses. Gates surround it along with being covered in cameras. The only one I've seen so far that has so much protection.

After a few minutes of standing there she comes out.

"Piddles!!!" She screeches and I make the kind of face you would at a New Kids on the Block concert. That's a modern reference isn't it? She hugs the thing, kisses it, and tells it how much she missed it.

I look up at Black, "can I get that ride now?"

In the car I can't help but focus my thoughts on the tape. Which I didn't tell Lurch about.

At this point I don't even care that I didn't get more money. You think they would have been able to have found that mutt easily on their own. If someone got their hands dirty and looked deeper within the kingdom in the sky. Instead of walking around handing out pieces of paper.

I'm pretty quiet the way home being distracted. The kid didn't come; she was too happy about the dog.

He stops in front of my building. I get out but before I close the door I turn and say "not even a thank you?" No response he keeps looking forward. "I didn't even say anything about not getting compensated." Before I could finish my sentence he drives off as I let go of the door. He zooms so fast the door closes on its own.

I get to the second floor and I'm presented with a tag on the opposite wall of my front door. It's a giant X, D on the top, E on the right, A on the bottom, and another D on the left. Ok fella's I get it, you and your big scary leader are still out there and I don't give a shit.

I get into my office. A long warranted sleep from a long unwarranted day. I'm too tired to drink. Hold your shock.

4

"No!" I scream out from my slumber. So much for a long peaceful sleep. Doesn't feel like I've been out for that long. This is why I don't go to bed sober.

I unleash myself out into the desolate streets to find nectar of the gods I call hutch. I come back happy, I drink happy. I eventually black out with a smile on my face, knowing I'm finally going to have a restful sleep.

I wake up a bunch of hours later eyes heavy but ready to take on alcohol. Aren't we done with this case? I found the dog. Oh wait, that's right the audio tape. I go to grab my coat and take the tape out of my pocket.

I leave my place and go to take the bus. On the bus heading to the electronics store I can't help but think how much I hate the bus.

Standing here getting stared at by everyone also helps me remember why. The passengers are creepy and the drivers are dicks. It's small and uncomfortable. It's literally like riding in a sardine can. Some kid's staring at me with his mouth open. I hate when brats do that shit. They look like Village of the Damned.

Got off the bus walking to the store. Thinking about children, I don't normally have a problem with them. The contempt I feel for them is equal to everyone else on this planet. That little girl was cool though. Most of them are not. Maybe that's why I don't care for them usually. Because they remind me of me.

I get to the electronic store fittingly called 'Automatic for the People'. I walk up to the cash register.

Behind it is a clerk standing with his back to me. I wait for him to turn around. He doesn't. I wait there a minute.

He finally does and says to me, "What!?!" In a real snide way.

"I'm looking for voice recorders." I say without reacting to his attitude.

"And!?!" He says while being very curt.

"Can you show me where they are?" Again, making sure this asshole does not cause me to react.

He lets out one of those big obnoxious sighs, almost a groan. "Fine!"

He brings me to the appropriate section and then leaves me there. He must be the employee of the month. I stand there for a few minutes in front of a wall of recorders.

I am overwhelmed and confused. I know technology but I'm a bit rusty with what's new. Staring at these things makes me feel like your mother trying to figure out Facespace or whatever it's called. A voice recorder seems simple enough, but some of these look straight out of Star Trek.

Finally, another clerk slides over eager to make a quick buck. He's much younger than the last one. Once I tell him what I'm looking for he veers the conversation into me getting a digital tape recorder.

Digital recorders mean no tapes. I try to explain this. He doesn't listen thinks I'm better off with digital. I try again to explain my situation.

Between each of his breaths, which are not many, I interject. As my attempts fall on literal deaf ears I quit. He won't listen and I stopped caring to try anymore. So I let him go through his pitch because lord knows he needs the practice.

After his long winded speech, he says "so which one will it be?"

I answer, "The one that takes cassettes." His smiling, pretentious persona starts to fade into a frown.

"Aw, don't seem so defeated. The older model that represents irrelevance is what I require for my situation. Not because I myself am old and inconsequential. It's more because this is what's necessary. Sometimes what you want isn't based on how you are. It's just what you need."

He points at what I was asking for. I pat him on his shoulder for a worthy but pointless job. I pay for the thing. As I'm leaving I tell the old nasty register person "thanks for the help, good luck getting that 5 cent raise."

He answers back "That's fine, I love it" with a huff. I exit the store.

Back at my place having to pass that tag before going into my office forces me to think of that foolish over-dramatic Hermano De Sangre. Too bad he's still alive. I take the cassette and put it in my new player. The sound starts off muffled. It starts to become clearer and I recognize that it's two men.

> **_Man one_**: *"How youse doin' Mr. Herodes, sit."*

> **_Man two_**: *"What is this about?"*

Man one: *"Would youse like anything to drink? Rondo, get our guest something stiff to loosen him up."*

Man two: *(says nervously)* *"Can we just move this along?"*

Man one: *"If dat's what youse want. I understand youse is building a new high rise on da east side. A great view of da river. Be da first of its kind. A masterpiece, 44 stories of dream living."*

Man one: *"It's very ambitious Mr. Herodes. I myself have been dabbling into da field of real estate."*

Man one: *"Whereas youse deal with da elite, I deal in da squalor. I'd like to make a deal as many men in our positions do. I sign on as youse partner in da deal. In doing so youse show me how to be a real estate mogul such as youseself." (A match can be heard being struck)*

Man two: (chuckles) "Are you serious? You really are delusional. You may have everyone fooled but not me. I see through your greedy façade. I have a thing called a board of directors in my company. I can't just sign you into the project. I'm not some, puppet master like you."

Man one: (puffs out smoke) "I assure youse I'm serious and I don't like to be mocked. I'm not greedy, I'm a futurist. I look towards da future to assure my own. I know youse have others in the company dat would raise an eyebrow. I suggest youse keep me as a silent partner." (Puffs out smoke)

Man two: "I am done listening to this. I knew when I heard you wanted to speak to me it would be pointless. I am not scared of you. You have nothing on me. You can't manipulate or intimidate your way this time." (Starts to get up)

Man one: "Rondo." (Commotion is going on)

Man two: "Hey! Let go of me!"

Man one: "Mr. Herodes, youse misunderstand me. Youse don't have a choice in dis. If we don't become partners I'll find someone in youse company who will understand da writing on da wall. The next in line perhaps."

Man one: "I understand that if anything were to happen to youse, God forbid, youse lovely daughter would take over. But, if anything tragic would ever happen to her, well…"

Man two: (sounds surprised) "Astra? You would hurt my little girl? She's all I have."

Man one: "I know. Youse wife died of breast cancer two years ago, very sad. Would be a shame to lose youse daughter too. Youse never know, accidents happen. Youse can lose everything without insurance. Rondo, why don't youse see Mr. Herodes to his car he has much to contemplate."

That seems to be the end of it. It goes silent for a while until the sound of a car door closing then it just stops altogether.

That was interesting to say the least. Obviously the second voice was Atticus Herodes. I've found out the answer to the question no one asked, her name is Astra. Now who is the first voice? Sounds like a real genius with all those 'youse' he was dropping. Still, it's similar to me just can't put my figurative finger on it.

That first voice sure knew a lot about Herodes. I'm zoning, who made that recording? Voice one sounded greedy as hell. I guess Herodes is pretty clean, from the surface.

Must figure out that Number one's voice I know I know it. It sounds like Mel from the Alice TV show. It's my only clue to finding Herodes and getting my McSrooge like pile of gold coins.

I leave my place. I walk the streets with my head half zoning. At first I decide to go to a bar just as the sun sets and creates a red haze over the sky.

Been going to bar's a lot lately. I guess it's because I had the money. Must stop soon since I gave most of it to the skipper. It's also a way to get out, to clear my head. A bar probably isn't the best place to do that sort of thing, but fuck it, it's my element.

Then I change my mind. I have the idea to blow out the rest of the money I still have. This is something I will most likely regret later on, but that's the story of my life. I celebrate nothing in style by doing something you never see me do, eat.

I need to go someplace where greasy food is a staple. Also having a bar is a requirement. I'll be able to drink as much as I want. Whatever terrible food I get will just constantly soak up the hutch.

That's why I've come up with, P. J. Hogsworth's Bacon Emporium. I am heading to a chain restaurant.

The commercials I've seen from other bars because I don't own a TV seem campy and dopey. So like a great place to make fun of. Plus, the entire menu has bacon in it. From bacon wrapped oysters to cheesecake with bits of bacon inside, this place has everything.

America loves thinly sliced smoke cured pig meat with more fat than meat fried up for that salty goodness. For an added bonus their mascot looks like a much fatter Colonel Sanders. Sometimes he'll wear his cotton suit jacket or just play with his suspenders like a stereotype on a Southern lawyer.

I get there and sit at the bar. I look around before the bartender comes over to me. It looks like a typical chain shithole.

They got crazy crap on the walls like street signs inside, whatever. I scan the menu and I've got the drink I want but now I need to pick a dish. There's bacon infused mozzarella sticks, bacon milkshakes, and tofu with bacon. That one is from the Vegetarian part of the menu, which seems to defeat the purpose.

Then there's an item that catches my eye, Hogwash. The menu says its pork flavored soda. This place is awesome, how the hell does it stay in business?

I order my hutch, the soda, and some mozzarella sticks. When I get my food I break it apart and the cheese stretches out with the bits of bacon inside. It seems like a lot of work just for an appetizer. It tastes as greasy as it sounds.

I have a few more plates of apps like bacon crusted chicken wings and bacon wrapped fried zucchini sticks. I think I have enough fatty crap in me to be close to being sober.

I finish with the food and start with the heavy drinking. This helps me relax and think about voice number one on that tape.

When I'm zoning I'll sometimes lose my concentration on the subject I started with. That's when my mind starts to wander.

There are a lot of sounds admitting around me. A collective chatter coming from the tables, horrible lite rock pouring out of the overhead speakers, a patron arguing with a manager, the news coming out of the TV.

Let me not forget the loon at the end of the bar screaming about the media controlling his libido. My natural curiosity is being enticed by all of them. Giving a crap with what's going around me isn't something I do normally anymore.

While in this state I am able to pick up these noises almost individually. The local news on the TV. Another scandal involving our esteemed Mayor. It wasn't what they were talking about but what he was saying that caught my ear.

The reporter was trying to be the hard hitting journalist she wished she was. She asked, "Mayor Loeb what do you say about the allegations that you were involved with the B6 crime spree real estate scam back when you were City Council president?"

Mayor Loeb's face is turning a shade of red as he starts to defend himself. I start to vaguely remember this scam. Along the old bus route of the B6 were a string of stores being robbed.

The cops found out the three guys committing the robberies were hired by someone. The crimes were supposed to bring down the property value. Therefore, whoever hired these guys would then buy the land cheap. A potential billion-dollar real estate scheme. Gimme me a break. It sounds like something from a shitty movie, like a sequel no less.

They never did find out who the mastermind was behind that because the three never confessed. It's been two years into his second term as Mayor and now new evidence has come to light pointing to Loeb. As he forms his words spit starts to form on the corner of his mouth.

The Mayor who looks a lot like Wilford Brimley and sounds like Mel from Alice was trying to defend himself. "Why do youse people always come to me wit every little rumor youse hears? When youse use real journalism and get some hard evidence, come back to me. I have a city to run."

I start to think, 'you mean to ruin'. I started chuckling to myself. Adding to the humor I thought, 'and what's up with the Soprano's accent'? Who says 'youse'? Then it dawned on me. The voice on the tape recorder, that's who. Holy crap, the Mayor was trying to extort from Herodes. The only question is why?

The rest of the night becomes a blur. This new nugget of information made me excited then it turned into depression. Although important it just becomes a way of drowning my sorrow.

The reason why is because I can't do anything with this. I don't have anywhere or anyone I can go that can use it. There's the paper but I need some more evidence before going to the next step. The hutch helps me forget.

5

I wake up in a stairwell. It smells like piss in here. I'm going to assume it's mine. I got to the blackouts last night so I didn't have dreams which is a pro.

I didn't check myself for mysterious cuts, bruises, or worse before passing out which is a con. I leave the housing project which for some reason I decided was a great place to sleep, I start thinking about the Mayor.

Turns out I have an idea of where I am. Walking to the nearest bus I'm trying to come up with a plan to meet his highness. Should I get him exposed to my captivating charm? Maybe he'll just find me? I could only be that lucky that I wouldn't have to lift a finger to get this meeting from happening.

I get to my office and crash on my couch. I'm still tired. Big surprise here since that was not the best sleep ever. As I slip into a nap I for once hope that trouble comes looking for me.

6

Problem is, that trouble does not come looking for me until a few months later. It's called a flash forward. I sat in my office, bored.

All I have to show for my time well spent is lesser empty bottles, a skinnier frame, and more hair on my face. I must trim it to get the 4:30 shadow look I like so much.

Without a good idea in my head, the rest of my money spent, or no new money coming in this really was a very uneventful two months. With peeing and eating sprinkled in-between.

I'm aware the explanation of those moments where I am doing those things has been pretty much nonexistent. I'm not a mannequin. It starts to dawn on me if only for a moment that Powers hasn't been around for his money lately.

During all that downtime I couldn't help but think about the Herodes girl. I know her dad's dead, so why do I still care? There's no incentive in going further.

I lie to myself into thinking it's to satisfy the inquisitive side to my personality. It's the truth that worries me. That I'm starting to have feelings again. I just hope it doesn't get worse.

I'm going to a sports bar tonight, Overtime. I don't go there because it's my scene but more for the bartenders. They are nice, yet stupid. The crowd sucks, just a bunch of knuckle dragging meatheads who love their football. It's the only place that will let me have a drink on credit. Like I said, nice yet stupid.

In the better part of town, I'm inside a bar filled with a bunch of guys who look like they might have been convicted of date rape. In between whatever dumbass college game that's playing is a commercial for the news.

The anchor did his thirty second promo mentioning the upcoming live footage of the ribbon cutting for the new Herodes residential skyscraper. I couldn't hear all of it because of the grunting and chanting that was going on in this cave.

While stealing some money off the bar that is intended for tips I leave.

I need it to familiarize myself with the most important source of information, a newspaper. Who am I kidding, it is not the most important source. Not since we had the ability to watch porn on our glasses. At this point it's all I could afford. Plus, there's no urinal's around. My real source for news.

Although, the library does have free internet but what do I look like, homeless?

Most of the print my eyes scan through is news to me. I'm so out of the loop about everything I still have an active Facespace account or whatever it's called.

There's an article about the ribbon cutting. It also explains that some weeks ago the so called 'police department' considered Herodes dead. Doesn't seem like enough time for the law to rule a missing person dead. Unless the one in charge was dirty. Fucking cops.

It goes on to say the head of the board was voted into being the acting CEO. Until the daughter is old enough to take over.

This sounds familiar, there's a very similar plot to a book on tape with the Mayor I was listening to a while back. Starting to get a twinge of worry for that little girl, have to ignore it.

The new CEO goes by the name of Jack Ryder. Paper confirms what the TV was saying that the ribbon cutting ceremony is in a few hours. Have to make a trip on the east side.

I'm zoning as I ride the bus antsy with anticipation. That kid's gonna be in danger soon if she isn't already. Unfortunately, that has to go on the back burner.

My main concern is this Ryder worm. I need to put the fear of God into him. Not too many people get intimidated by me. Then again as a cartoon once taught me as a kid, knowledge is power. My zoning is too deep I almost miss my stop.

When I get off the bus I do my best of hustling to the spot of the new building. What I mean by 'hustle' is just a tad faster than my normal walking. I hate running, try to avoid it at all costs. I could step on a nail and not know.

I get to the spot. Right off the water, breath taking view. No wonder the Mayor wants a piece of this. The building is shiny and tall. Reporters, supporters, and on lookers make up the large mass of people surrounding this thing. There's even a make shift stage with a banner and an actual ribbon. They really do that?

Someone introduces Ryder who then walks up on stage and to the mic. He's a skinny smarmy kind of guy. Not so much Gargamel smarmy, more like someone who would sell out their Grandma for a lollipop. Ooh, I could go for one of those right now. I don't see any kids around, now who seems smarmy?

Ryder, who's wearing a suit with a black band around the upper part of his left arm. His attire suggests he's trying hard not to look smarmy.

He starts to speak into the mic. "Thank you all very much for coming. I know Atticus would have been humbled to have seen everyone here today. This was his baby and it saddens me to know he's not here to see his baby being born. I know in my heart he's looking down and sharing this experience with all of us."

Way to acknowledge you believe he's dead even further. "Once again, thank you all for coming. Without further ado may I present the Atticus Herodes memorial tower!"

He turns around facing the ribbon that was behind him. Someone runs up on stage to hand him the abnormally large red scissors.

I notice the Mayor's not around. Neither is Herodes daughter. Ryder cuts the ribbon, people cheer, and he's smiling. I start to make my move. I try to make it closer to him as quick as I can. I make it through the flock of sheep known as citizens. It's the gaggle of egotistical reporters I know will be a challenge to get through.

I try my best but a meathead cameraman and the whorish looking reporter with way too much makeup on are in my way and won't move. It's a wall of cameras.

I get the idea to kick the back of the cameraman's knee. When I do it causes him to jolt forward which then hits the female reporter with the camera. This causes a chain reaction as she then hits into the poor excuse of a journalist standing next to her.

With the expensive camera smashed on the floor both reporters get into a fight. The one thing a reporter hates is when you get into their shot. This gets the attention of the security surrounding Ryder.

As I step through the hole in the mass of cameras I just created I get as close as I can, stopping at the steel barricade. With Ryder standing on the other side I try to get his attention. "Psst, hey, Mr. Ryder." He can hear me but doesn't react.

"I got this great book on tape. It's about a Mayor murdering a wealthy real estate mogul. Then the Mayor sets up the head of the board of directors to take the dead mogul's place. This charlatan gets in bed with the Mayor so they could share the profits of a new building the mogul's company built."

"Meanwhile the Mayor and the charlatan plot to kill the mogul's daughter, who's really in line to head her daddy's company."

I said all this as quickly as I could all the while embellishing just a bit. His expressive reaction is priceless though. All the color leaves his face turning it pale. He then looks around to make sure none of the twenty reporters around me heard what I just spilled.

They didn't, everyone's too busy with the battle of the egomaniacs.

I finish it off by saying "how do you think my book on tape will end? I think the charlatan will get exposed by the spunky, heroic protagonist." I smile wide while pointing at myself.

Then he looks at me and slowly nervously walks over. He starts to sweat and he stutters as he speaks. "Wha- What do you- do you know?"

I smirk as I answer. "I know you're just a pawn. I know that what I hold in my possession can bring this whole thing crashing down. I'm looking for fatter fish to fry." God, I sound as cliché as these fools.

"Tomorrow, get me a meeting with the fat man. My terms, Ole Water Hole, 72 E 2nd street. It's discreet and in a way different neighborhood than this, let's say 10pm."

He shakes his head with a frighten look. I leave and head to the bus station. I'm pretty proud of myself, I deserve a drink. Maybe I'll go down to my new favorite sports bar Strike Zone again and take advantage of my new favorite bartender.

That's what I decide to do. I leave when I'm on the brink of the blackouts. I can't believe I'm happy with myself. I really am getting sucked into this Marlowe crap. I'm getting as bad as the rest of the nuts I deal with. Especially Blood, I would die happy if I never have to deal with that loon again.

I'm opening the door to my office and I'm still smiling on the high created chemically and from my own self-worth.

That grin gets wiped off my face when I see the behemoth standing in my office. His hairy hands that look like they could rip phone books in half grabs me by my face. As I slip into the blackouts against my own will the one thing I keep thinking, 'how do people keep breaking into my office'?

7

My eyes open slowly. I'm face deep in a leather couch. The black leather is cool on my skin. Head feels heavy as I try to lift it. The couch sticks to my face as I notice I drooled as I slept. I start thinking about that guy.

To call him a man is offensive to all men. He had the size and frame of Frankenstein's monster. He had a face that a mother would not love, she would try to drown it.

I sit up, I notice an empty desk in the middle of the room. I also notice the big lug with the harsh face standing to my right. He's wearing the same get up I saw him in before. A long black trench coat, with a matching fedora.

"Is our guest waking from his beauty sleep?" A voice comes from a room behind the big guy. "Rondo, show him in and remember youse manners."

The giant grabs me from my collar and pulls up. He pushes me into the room. It's a big round office with windows looking onto the hollow lights of the city.

The enormous oak desk is directly in front of the view. A slightly obese man with multiple chins is sitting behind it. It's the Mayor. On top of his sweaty forehead are white hairs in a terrible comb over.

His desk is covered with a plethora of an assortment of foods, a real buffet. He stuffs his cheeks with chow.

A napkin wrapped around his girthy neck catches every morsel that sloshes out of his sloppy mouth. Which is quite often. Every once and a while he will push his glasses in leaving a grease shimmer on the bridge.

The colossus with the face that looks like he had acid thrown at him forces me to sit in a lone chair facing the desk.

The Mayor is multitasking with the eating. One hand has a fried chicken leg while the other has a cheeseburger. When the burger is done the empty hand swoops down like an eagle to grab the next course. This time it's a corn on the cob.

"The infamous Champ I presume. I hear youse have something we'd be interested in. What did youse call it, a 'book on tape'"? I guess my plan sort of backfired. It got me a meeting with the Mayor though. "Do youse have dis amazing piece of literature on youse?"

"No, I do not." I'm not lying it's in my office. "Have you thought about getting a speech therapist to look at that horrible accent of youse? Do you know how embarrassing it is when people find out you're from this city? That your mayor is Super Mario? That's why I never admit where I live. Bad enough it's a crime ridden cesspool."

The behemoth is about to hit me when Boss Hogg orders him not to. "I am a powerful man. I advise youse not to get in bed with da King Cobra. He will fill youse wit poison." The chicken leg has been replaced with a lamb shank.

I start to laugh. "You think you're as powerful as a cobra? It's more like you're as overweight as an elephant. The only power you have is in your ass with the threat of sitting on people."

"Dat isn't fat on the elephant, its mass used as muscle. And I assure youse dat is what youse see here, mass and muscle." He says as he stuffs his face with hot garbage.

I laugh so hard I almost fall out of my chair. "Ok, give me the change to hit you in your giant round area of muscle. Well see if it bounces off or if you'll just swallow my arm. By the way you may want to loosen your collar. It looks like it's choking on your chins."

He stops gorging himself as he points his half eaten lamb shank at me. "Youse humor me Mr. Champ" says Henry the VIII. He starts to speak again while putting the lamb back into his mouth. "Or should I say, Mr. Leonard Champowski."

I stop laughing. My forehead turns into a wrinkled brow. My eyes have started the evil gaze. If there was anything in the world that would get me to shut up it would be someone saying my full name.

This is something I try very hard to hide. If you know my name you either know me or you looked into one of my many files. I don't know too many people who still know my name, so it has to be the latter.

Needless to say, color me shocked. "I see that has shut youse up. Son, youse haven't heard anything yet. You have stumbled onto something so massive dat youse tiny head will explode when we're done here's." A filet mignon has replaced the cob.

I don't say anything. I just sit there with my brow still scrunched, color me intrigued. "Leonard Champowski, I doubt I have to tell youse the date of youse birth. Born to Peter and Mary Champowski."

"Youse have **Congenital Analgesia**, terrible condition. Not being able to feel pain caused youse to bite the tip of youse tongue off when youse were nine months old. Aw, dat's terrible. Can youse open up youse mouth, I wanna get a look."

He's not reading this off of anything. He just keeps double fisting the food as he talks. He stops when he wants to see my tongue, I don't give him the satisfaction. "No, well I could just make Rondo do it for youse. But I don't think I will. I do wanna see da Analgesia in action. Rondo if youse will."

The big gallop catches me with a right fist in the face. I jerk but my facial expression doesn't change. I'm starting to figure that this must be the guy who grabbed and possibly murdered Herodes. Color me angry.

"And youse don't feel anything, dat's amazing. I'm sure dat thing comes in handy sometimes." He's talking about my condition like it's a mutant power. This guy is on some power trip shit, what a dick. Color me annoyed.

He goes back to eating, "allow me to continue with what I was talking about. At da age of eight while in da third grade youse had a bit of an accident at school. While in da gym period youse broke youse ankle."

"It happened's, but da problem was youse didn't know at da time. Youse discovered it a few hours later, very sad."

"Youse mutter, being over protective as she should have been with a boy in youse condition, pulled youse from school. She had youse home schooled all the way to High School. Must have been hard growing up not being able to do what da other kids could. I'm sure friends were pretty non-existent."

"What's the point of this trip down memory lane? So you read a file on me, who gives a shit. I know what I did, I fucking did it. If you're going to intimidate me, intimidate me, shit or get off the pot fat fuck." Color me fed up.

He stops eating, "youse bored or something?" He looks up at the looming shadow that hangs over me. "Why don't we get to da juicy part then, huh, Rondo?" I hear a dumb 'yuck yuck' laugh behind me. He goes back to gorging.

"I'll skip da part when you joined da academy shortly after College. I'm sure youse mutter wasn't too happy about dat. Youse lied about your medical problem. But youse were very careful whenever it came to da physical stuff."

"You came top of youse class. A few years on da force youse made Junior Detective and put in for Robbery. One of the quickest climbs ever in the history of da force, very impressive."

Right now I close my eyes and I brace myself. Color me worried for the simple fact that I had a feeling he was going down this road. Don't say his name, please don't say his name, not like this.

"Da is when youse were partnered up wit a Charles Polletti," fat ass said. As his name passed his lips my teeth clenched, my eyes were shut tight, and my face turned red.

"Da two of youse became pretty close. Partners for seven years, impressive. I myself have never had a partner. I do knows dat when youse a part of this city's finest it makes youse part of a brotherhood. And as youse two became closer, youse stumbled onto somethings."

I'm in a cold sweat with my eyes glued shut. I know he's trying to get a rise out of me. I can't help but react in any other way. This is my nightmare coming true. Color me panicking.

"Cops on da take something youse couldn't handle. Charles had been dealing wit it before youse signed on. He was living wit it. He may not have agreed but what could he do?"

"Youse on the other hand, God forbid youse play ball. Youse think I'm reading this from a file. Something that was written by a guy behind a desk who claims to be a cop? I'll tell youse something that was never on any report."

The sweating gets worse, it's because I'm in hell. I start rocking trying to deflect this shit. I yell with my eyes clamped closed "shut up shut up shut up!" Color me fractured.

He ignores me and keeps going. "I've got a good idea for a story for youse, it's a story about two cops who couldn't keep dere noses where dey didn't belong."

"One of them, years of experience under his belt. He knew how to play da game, where he fit in da order of dings. Sure, maybe he was a coward for sitting on his hands for all dose years. Or maybe dat made him smart, made him wise. Let's not forget da beautiful family he had to think about."

I stopped rocking and open my eyes with the mention of the word 'family'. I try to forget them every day.

"Da other cop is self-righteous, headstrong, stubborn, and a bit of a loner. No one seems to like him but he doesn't care. He's got a chip on his shoulder and he can't wait to take it off and shove it up someone's ass. Dat hot feeling in da pit of the cocky cop's stomach seems to subside when dey become partners. For a while at least."

"It eventually comes back when he finds out about da department's dirty little secret in da take backs. When da older, wiser cop tells da younger, cocky cop to lay off he don't listen. Even after dere threatened da younger cop doesn't back off."

I put my hands over my ears. Color me in denial.

"Rondo would youse please." My arms are pinned down to my sides. "Until da day da younger cop is taken from his bed at night. With a bag over his head and hands tied behind his back he still fights never admitting defeat."

"When da traveling stops and da bag removed da younger cop recognizes where he is. It's da house of his partner which he had visited quite often as he was an honorary member of da family."

"When he looks around in da dark for dis family he has grown to love, something he never thought he could do, he don't find dem. Dat's when he looks down and discovers dem in a pool of dere own blood. Mother, and ten-year-old twins, a boy and a girl, adorable kids from what I heard."

"All laying in da red slick goo dat once poured out of dem. Along with his partner, dere father and husband, da young cop just stares."

As he relates my own bleak history to me I try to ignore as best as I can. He still continues to stuff his fat mouth as he talks but I don't notice what he's eating anymore. I have cemented my eyelids shut.

I can only imagine he's still spitting out crumbs as he does his best Bond villain impression. If he were a Bond villain his name would be, Fatfinger.

Everything he says cuts deep but I will not cry for this fat bastard. This is what he wants. I try to hold it back. Like a crack in a dam the tears start to trickle out. I never whimper though. Color me ashamed.

"When da masked men behind him try to shove his face in da mess he helped create he resists. Da men give him an ultimatum, probably da most important decision in his life. Either give up dis ridiculous obsession or become da number one suspect in da murder of da Polletti family. He gave his answer to leave it alone, a smart move."

"But in case he would forget his promise, da men left him with a Polaroid picture. A Polaroid, how dated, but it made its point. Da last family picture of da Polletti's along with da young cop. A picture dat speaks a thousand words. Do youse still have da picture I wonder?"

With my head down I slowly wipe the tears from my cheeks. I don't say anything at first. My head starts to rise staring up at him I calmly say, "you know I do you fat fuck." I put my head back down.

"I imagine youse would. Da rest of da story isn't as exciting. Da young cop leaves da force due to 'mental stress'. Caused by da brutal murder of da partner and his family. Which by the way was committed by a drug addict dat da older cop once busted. He died for dat crime, justice prevails after all."

"Da young cop spends some time in a mental facility for a while. He comes out a changed man. Yes, a changed, bitter, angry man. Den he decides to be a private detective."

I lift my head up again. With an angry look on my face and all my bottled emotions on that night come pouring out. I start to scream. "Joke's on you, I was already bitter." My humor that helps deflect my true emotions prevail, if barely.

I go on, "what's the point of this? Is this your way of trying to intimidate me? You think this trip down memory lane will inspire me to do 'the right thing' again!? Your twisted version of the right thing?"

"Well fuck you fat man that is not going to happen! You dredging this shit up just makes me want to shove that cassette tape I have down your fucking throat!!"

He stops eating, puts his hands flat on his desk, stands up, and starts yelling with pieces of food spitting out of his mouth.

"Youse don't get it, hell son, nuttin' in dis town happens without my say-so! I ordered the hit on dat family. I ordered youse exile. Youse fucked up psyche, youse loner existence, and the reason why youse a drunk loser is because of me!!"

I shake my head with my eyes tight again. Then I open them to yell again. "No you don't get it, I was already a loser. All you did was force me to realize what I had wasn't really mine to begin with." I will not let him break me with his 'revelation.'

He ignores my recent outburst and sits back down. "Let me introduce youse to someone, Rondo?" The big moron leaves me and goes to the front office to open a door. He comes back with someone who stands behind me that I can't see them. "Son, meet Det. Simbudyal, but you may already know him as-"

I turn around and connect my eyes with the eyes of this new player. I feel as if I've been kicked in the chest as my heart and breathing has stopped.

My whole body freezes as I start to whisper with my last breath, 'Fucking Powers.' I sit there fixated on him. With my face still frozen from shock he just stands there smirking. This is how he knew my full name. A crooked cop working with the Mayor. I start to wonder if he had anything to do with that night.

The Mayor speaks as if he just read my mind. "In case youse was wondering Det. Simbudyal or 'Derek Powers' as youse know him, was in fact da one dat took dat Polaroid. Dat last piece of memory youse have."

Words are pouring out of his mouth but I don't pay attention. I keep staring at Powers or whatever his name is and he keeps staring back. He's still smirking and his eyes have grown wide with glee. It's almost as if he's enjoying this.

"I put him on youse detail, to follow and watch youse." The Mayor's words still have no meaning to me. Those eyes, wide with enjoyment, that's all that's important to me. I bet he couldn't wait to spring this on me. The secret he was just dying to let out.

My body starts to get hot. Everything inside me from my brain, plasma, organs, and my cells scream at once for Power's blood.

I rise from the chair, swerve around with rage on my mind. Nothing matters but Powers and what I was going to do to him. Color me enraged. I might have screamed, but I don't remember. I'm pretty sure drool was involved.

When we go through experiences, even those that last seconds, our brains can process so much information. Like thoughts for example. How many times have you had a millions things run through your mind but as a real time moment just lasted two seconds?

This was not one of those times. All I heard in my mind was 'kill', over and over. His death would not subdue or even extinguish my guilt. As long as I am alive and the earth turns I will always have that.

A physical and emotional weight, like wearing a concrete block. All killing him will do is fulfill a small need of punishing just one of the many factors responsible with the clusterfuck I know I created.

I decide to participate in my carnal desires anyway. As I lunge for Powers my thirst for revenge is denied as these two tree trunks slam down on my shoulders. "Now now son, we don't want to do anything too rash to our guest." Sure I do, I want to kill him. Powers is laughing. The more he still exists the more I want him dead.

"I'll never forget that night, you were a crying sniveling little homo like you are now." For the record, I stopped tearing as soon as that trash stepped into the room.

The Mayor stops eating and takes a napkin that was his bib covered in food crap and wipes his sloppy mouth. "Dis is what youse will do, bring me dat tape, or we will find...what's that girls name?" He asks as he points his sausage finger at Powers.

"Astra," Powers answers back quickly, smiling. I keep trying to turn my head too look at the prick but only get glimpses since the big gallop does an excellent job of pinning me down.

"That's it and youse ex-girlfriend, uh," once again points at Powers. For someone who remembered my file so well he's doing a shit time trying to remember the people in my life.

"Sarah," says the wormy fuck as he then smirks. Powers adds salt, "that's a nice piece of ass, how you ever got her is beyond me. Maybe I'll try to pipe that and send you a picture to jerk off to." Everyone laughs, even Rondo who I doubt knows what's going on. His attempt on intimidation colors me furious.

The Mayor places a hand on top of a wooden box that's laying on his desk. He takes out a cigar among many. He pulls out a hundred-dollar bill, lights the bill, and then begins to light the cigar with it.

Is this motherfucker actually lighting up a cigar with money? I'm too doped up on emotions to make a smart crack about how much of a stereotypical gangster movie crime boss he looks like.

"Rondo, please escort our friend outside. Don't forget son, I want dat tape. Or else, you will see your loved ones in a river of blood, make dat smart decision again."

As the mongoloid picks me up and pushes me out the door I finally snap out of it and say, "joke's on you, I don't have any loved ones."

Heading out the door Powers gives me that devilish look and grin and says, "See you soon tenant." I immediately try to lunge at him but am stopped mid-way.

Rondo throws me out onto the street literally. I'm too frazzled with anger to check for any major wounds. I can't go home and stew in my own juices. I need some release.

I'm too outraged to drink and too wired with my hatred to sleep. Everything that just happened mixed with pieces of my past keep replaying in my head. It causes the rage to suppress but brings out the guilt in its place. Dwelling on the guilt then brings back the rage. It all becomes a vicious cycle.

Having a release will help me not kill Powers or the Mayor the next time I see either one. I want to do what overly aggressive men do, not sex, but brawl.

I go to a bar and without wasting much time pick a fight. I don't even come up with a snappy wise crack to make to anyone. I just turn to a guy to my right and say "whatever loved one you hold close to your heart is a whore."

That gets the job done. Problem is, he was with a group. I got a few licks in but in the end, I am on the floor covering myself.

Story of my life. Still, I'm getting pretty tired of always ending a fight on the floor. I was lucky only walked away with some bruised ribs and a swollen cheek. It is what I needed though, the fight not the bruises. I get home, I drink, and then I sleep. It's been a long and terrible day.

8

I wake up and decide despite my better judgment to call Sarah. I need to warn her about the Mayor and Powers. That's a lie, what I really need is

Power's info. The part of me that ignores everyone's feelings is locked in a closet like R. Kelly. The caring part is free and leaning on the door. He hasn't been out and about in a long time.

My guilt rises from the dark part in my gut and it wants me to turn this phone call into a 'spill my guts out' session. I am apprehensive about that. I'm not one to indulge my problems or past on people, not even people I used to date.

I start to dial her work number, when no one answers I realize the time and how late it is. I must not have slept for that long. In fact, I think I'm still drunk. I hang up and start her home number. It dawns on me that I haven't remembered that number in forever until right now. I hope she hasn't changed it.

A groggy hello answers the phone when I think how I'm glad she hasn't. I start talking fast, "Sarah, I know it's late but I need your help." T

Here are things I strive to try not to do. Putting myself out for others is one, buying milk that's close to being expired is another. But the one thing I can't do, I won't do, not anymore is, "I'm sorry Sarah," apologize.

"What"? She asks groggy and confused. "Why are you bothering me? I was sleeping."

"I know, I just wanted to apologize for being such a fuck these past few years." My head says I'm doing the right thing by apologizing. I know I'm really just buttering her up so I can ask her to do something that could get her fired.

"I need to, explain a few things. I want to tell you something that I've been keeping from you. I have **Congenital Analgesia**; I cannot perceive pain."

"My mother didn't know until I was almost a year old. I had bit down on my tongue without knowing it. I took the tip right off. I have a slight speech impediment. I'm sure you might had noticed. It would have been worse had my mother not sent me to a speech coach as soon as I could talk. It made growing up difficult to say the least."

"By the way, I say 'mother' and not 'parents' isn't because I was raised by a single parent. It's because my father although married to my mother, never acted as a parent. He was like a set piece in a movie, he was just there."

"I'm sorry," she says sounding sincere. "But that doesn't excuse your behavior. The last time we spoke was years ago when you left the force. And the things that you said weren't exactly sweet. 'You're a controlling cunt' I believe was one of them."

Damn, that's going to be hard to be forgiven for and I know that wasn't the worse of it. "Another greatest hit was I'm just some cooze good enough for piping. All I wanted to do was help but all you did was push me away. It wasn't until my phone rang a few months ago that we started talking again. You hurt me bad."

Another notch on the guilty belt. "I know and I'm sorry. That was right after," I hesitate saying their name, "they died. I was messed up." This is partly true; the other reason is I was afraid she would be next but I can't tell her that. Or how Charlie, Tina, and the kids are my fault. I went through a downward spiral so fast it was more like a slide.

She tried so hard to reach out, to help, but I was so afraid about her being a target. So I broke up with her, on the phone. I didn't know now or then what I was saying. "Speaking of them I know who did it." I decide to get to the point and deflect this part of the conversation.

"What are you talking about," she asks confused. "They caught the asshole who did it, Manny Balestrero and he was executed for it. A drug addict who wanted revenge for Charlie collaring him years ago."

"No, it wasn't Balestreo," I inform her. "He was a common thief and a drug addict. Killing four people with one of them being a seasoned veteran cop. Then to drag all those bodies down a flight of stairs, not to mention burning the house down. Doesn't that seem like a lot of work for one petty criminal who wasn't the killer?"

"He wasn't even that good of a criminal. In and out of prison so many times and never pulled off something that big on his own. How could he even remember Charlie being his arresting officer almost twenty years before the murders? He was the wrong man."

"I get it though, when something atrocious happens to someone, especially when it's somebody you love it's easy to accept any answer.

Even if that answers wouldn't make sense seen through a clearer head."

"When twin ten year olds you watched grow up and called you 'uncle' get brutally murdered a simple thing like common sense gets throw out the window. That's what they wanted everyone to think. Add to the fact that they burned down the house so it became harder to collect evidence."

Case in point, they couldn't prove the point of origin when it came to where they were murdered. Will she figure out how I know they were dragged down the stairs before I tell her, which will not be now.

"Who's they," she's says confused again.

I swallow my emotions and just tell the story. "It was Lieutenant Wulf, well I don't know if he was involved but I always expected. I do have proof that a cop was there that night."

Wulf was in our department, Robbery. He was a cocky fuck. Not a 23-year old who just became detective and thinks he knows everything about the world kind of cocky. More like he could punch the pope in the face and get away with it.

"What makes you think Wulf was there? What proof do you have?"

I do not want to get into detail about this now. "You have corrupt cops in your precinct Sarah. I cannot go into the how's or whys this very moment. I know I have not earned your trust back yet. You have to believe me though."

"I promise I will tell you everything." I'm hoping this will work. I will tell her the truth, just not for a while. A long while.

"I don't know what to say, this is a wild accusation your making."

"I know Sarah, also the Mayor set it up."

She's surprised, "wait, what," she asks puzzled and in total shock.

"Yeah, I don't know details yet but you have to believe me. Remember I said I was sorry." I half smirk even though she won't see it.

"This is a lot to digest."

"I know. Look I just need you to look into a name for me. His name his Powers." It dawns on me that's not his name. "Wait, no, that's not it, it's..."

I'm trying to remember, my memory used to be better. What was it? I think back, as much as I don't want to replay that particular memory. Then like a firework in my head I suddenly got it, "Simbudyal, Det. Simbudyal."

"I don't know; I could get into a lot of trouble for this. The risk is too great. Besides what's the evidence you have on this? How would the Mayor be involved?" She sounds skeptical.

I need to give her something other than my words because that means shit right now not that I blame her. I decide to play on the heart strings. "Please Sarah, don't do it for me, do it for Charlie, Tina, and the twins."

I'm pulling out a real cliché move right now. It's real scummy I know, but I'm desperate. I shouldn't do this. If I want her to trust me I have to give her a reason to. "I have an audio tape."

"Of what," she asks interested.

I put it on the line. "It's a conversation between the Mayor and Atticus Herodes the philanthropist. As you know he's been missing for a while. He's been declared dead, a little too quickly I think. The Mayor clearly threatens him on the tape."

So I play it for her. Afterword's I don't get an immediate response. A few seconds pass then all she can say is "wow" in a low tone.

"Yeah," is all I can say. "Herodes made it knowing the Mayor was up to something. This Simbudyal is a connection to that and Charlie."

I put up a good case now let's hear the verdict. After a few seconds of deciding what's more important revenge or her job she answers me. "Ok, I'll take a look when I get into work."

"Thank you," I respond with another phrase I don't like giving out to people.

"Look at you trying to do the noble thing." That comment stings a little because if she only knew all of my actions are originally based on selfishness.

Everything I told her was sincere though. Despite the fact that what I told her was just so she could do something for me. The talk I have with her to lift the emotional baggage I carry will come much later.

I begrudgingly thank her again then hang up. Still reeling from the emotional damage of a few days ago, I drink heavily. Then the blackouts come.

9

I wake up from having a dream. Not the typical kind of dream that's more like a nightmare. This one was a bit more calming. Still it's odd that I even had one since I drank enough to knock an ox out, for a week.

It takes me a minute to realize the phone is ringing. I slowly pick up the receiver. It's Sarah and she's talking low.

"I found out our friend's info." Her trying to speak inconspicuously is adorable.

"What did you find out?" I ask her.

"First, you were right." Words I love to hear. "His real name is Khan Simbudyal. He's a ten year veteran, works in Vice."

Vice, that makes sense. It's hard to wash the crud off that comes with working in that shithole. "What about his address?"

"I was getting there. Listen to this, he lives in Kingsbridge." Shit, that's one step below living in a gated community like Kalani. Being the Mayor's errand boy must pay well.

Sarah gives me his address, 1921 Severin Street. She asks me what I'm going to do. I tell her, "We're going to talk about our favorite Bond. I will say mine is George Lazenby, then we'll discuss."

She then says to not do anything that would get me in trouble. I say calmly, "as long as Mr. Powers cooperates, I'll be a good boy, mom." I have become a stereotype, it's sickening.

I decide to mentally prepare myself before I go hunting. When I say 'prepare' I mean get some Hutch and go to the blackouts. I drink whatever I have left in the office. As I drain my supply I think to myself, 'what am I going to do when I get to Powers'?

My eyes start to get blurry and heavy. When everything goes fade to black I answer myself, 'I have no fucking clue'.

10

The next morning is a productive one. I sink shower, and put on some clean clothes. I have to look and smell good if I'm going to intimidate. On the other hand, I guess smelling bad might help getting answers out of people. Also having a blade in your possession helps too. I go through my desk to find it. Have had it for a while, barely used it.

Powers, or Simbudyal, lives in Kingsbridge which is pretty much a suburban neighborhood. Fortunately, there is a bus stop near his house.

While on the bus I'm zoning thinking about the Mayor and how Powers fits into all this.

Owning my building fits in somehow and I'm starting to think so does that high-rise Herodes was building. Along with that scam the Mayor pulled when he was in City Council that their still trying to bust him on.

I know my questions will be answered soon, I just don't know how far I'll go after I get them.

I get off the bus and head to the corner just around his house. I stand there as his place is in my view. It's the morning time people are busy getting ready for the day. Hopefully they won't notice a creepy guy hanging around the corner.

The front of his house opens and he walks out with a little girl and a woman, his wife and daughter I'm assuming. He kisses them right before they get into a white car that's parked in the driveway.

Powers waves to them as they drive off. He then goes back inside. The car drives past as I back away so they don't notice me. I don't know if he has the day off or if he's going into work soon, so I have to do this now.

I turn the corner and cross the street. I look down at both sides of the road. While putting on rubber gloves I got on the way here I walk up his front porch. It's hard to explain how I'm feeling at this moment. I still don't know what I'm going to do, I only hope my emotions don't get the best of me too much.

I knock on the door which is made of a white wood and has a glass window in the middle. I hide from the window when he asks who it is. I say, "Girl Scout cookies," without even trying to hide my voice.

"What," he seems confused as he opens the door. His face is frozen with shock as his eyes meet mine. Everything seems to go in slow motion as I notice his right hand go for the glock in his left shoulder holster. I raise my fist and clock him in the face before he can fully grip his gun.

As he falls back onto his expensive looking marble floor I slowly walk into his house closing the front door behind me. I climb on top of him sitting on his stomach. He's holding his nose, I made a good shot. I take his gun out of his holster and throw it behind me.

I check my hand quick to make sure it's not broken. I get close to his face and ask calmly, "is there anyone else in the house?"

He's in pain and although he's not screaming he's making enough noise where he didn't hear me. I grab his arm and hit him in the nose with his own hand and politely ask him again. This time he screams, "No!"

I speak without getting upset. "This is how it's going to go down. You will tell me everything about the Mayor and your involvement with Charlie's murder."

He screams back, "Fuck you!"

I sigh in response. Then I tell him, "I was hoping this would go a lot smoother. You know about my 'condition'. You know that I don't feel pain."

I smack him to make sure he's paying attention. "I can produce a lot of pain for you for a very long time. What this means is I can go a while without feeling any effects from beating you. No pain for me means a lot more pain for you. Tell me about the Mayor."

He answers me by spitting in my face which is now mixed with blood from his broken nose. I will not get angry. I will not let my emotions get the best of me. Frankly, I don't care enough to be upset. I need info and I'm going to get it by any means necessary. I knew he would be difficult.

While still sitting on him I take a big bounce right on his stomach. It causes him to go, "oof!"

I get up and while he's still winded from playing bouncy castle on his wittle tummy I force him to stand up. He doesn't try to fight back until I get behind him and administer a choke hold.

I calmly wrap my right arm around his throat and lock in place with my left. More pressure gets dispensed when he applies more resistance.

He starts to blackout. The determined look on my face as I do this reminds me of a sociopath. Things are about to get Hostel up in this bitch.

I wake him up by setting his nose. It gets him to scream, more like a howl. I've taken tissues and plugged up his bleeding nostrils.

He's sitting in one of his dining table chairs. Nice work, thick wood, and very sturdy. I tied his wrists to the arms of the chair with his shoelaces. I took his handcuffs and attached it to his ankles.

His belt is around his neck choking him as the other end is tied to his lovely staircase banner. I also cleaned up my face while he was out by wiping it on his shirt.

To stop his howling, I slap him. "Let's start with, what do you do for the fat man?" He responds by saying he is going to kill me. "Too late, you already had a part in that."

I punch him in the right side of his face. He starts to scream in pain but stops to cough. Because of the tissue in his nose he has a hard time breathing. That was the plan all along.

I stand behind him and grab his wet hair due to his sweating and pull back. Looking down at his eyes filled with fear I speak to persuade him. "Pain makes us weak, it stops a man from achieving his goals. Pain creates fear which then creates an all-around weak person."

"One can never persevere through the toughest challenges that life throws at us when dealing with these two emotions. The heroes are the ones who look at pain and without so much as a flinch keep going. They say 'not today or any other day pain, you will not make me your slave.'"

"Looking back at your life if you can honestly say 'I did this in the face of pain', then that is a true accomplishment. That makes you a man and even in death, this makes you a winner."

Blood's words coming out of my mouth. "You will never be this kind of man. Now that last smack was a warning, fuck with me again and the pain will be worse." I say all of this in my monotone sociopath voice.

He struggles to look at me when his head his jerked so far back. "That pussy was so tight while your partner whined like a little bitch."

I don't react, I let go of his hair. Moving in front of him I grab the first finger on his right hand. Then I push it towards him fast and hard. His screams are high pitch and whiney, "did he sound anything like that?"

His bellowing makes me roll my eyes and creates contempt on my face.

I've never experienced physical pain. I'd like to think I wouldn't react in this way. Most of my pain has been the emotional kind. Which is different and equally terrible. Although a broken finger is pretty fucking bad.

"You people think I'm weak. That I'm some broken man you created and now you can walk all over me. You have it all wrong. I choose to live the way I do because I don't care. You are the broken one, you are the shell of a man that is hollow inside. I know who I am, do you know who you are?"

He tries to retort. "Fu...fu...fu...fuck...yu...," with a mix of blood, sweat, tears, and drool he can't quite get it out.

"Oh I'm sorry you can't seem to keep up your tough persona right now? Bottom line you don't tell me what I want to know, I am breaking your middle finger. The next word out of your mouth better be either about your role in all of this, the Mayor's role in all this, or you're going to have two finger splints."

"No...no...please." The pain might have broken him. My lack of sympathy for him causes me to break his middle finger. This all may seem excessive but I have to break him down. He represents that alpha male persona a lot of guys portray that's just utter bullshit.

After more screaming his head falls down with all of his body fluids dripping out of his face. I slap him in the back of the head. Then like hitting the side of a TV when it's not working, he just perks right up and his mouth starts flowing out the info.

"The mayor has a personal death squad, their all cops." He says as he breathes heavily between every other word.

Calling me confused would be an understatement. "What the fuck does that mean?"

He explains further. "He's surrounded himself with a team of cops he personally chose as his honor guard, his inner circle. He started scouting as soon as he started his first term. There are ten of us. It started off for us to make some money on the side."

The more he continues I'm convinced I did break whatever was inside of him that wouldn't comply.

"We began small like protection rings or taking profits from dealers and pimps in exchange for not busting them. With the Mayor getting a bigger piece. Then he informed us he had bigger plans. He wanted to expand the 'business', but into some legitimate ventures." He keeps coughing and breathing heavy as he talks.

This is too important and the last piece of my puzzle. So I let him go uninterrupted. I will not interject with sarcastic asinine comments.

"My partner and I shook down the dealers. The Mayor came to us about expanding. He had the idea to go into different fields. My partner was to go fully into drugs, to deal with distribution. He wanted me to deal with real estate. I'm in so much pain."

"Yeah I feel bad for you," I say as I roll my eyes a bit. Then I ask him, "was Wulf a part of this?"

He breathes heavy before answering. "Yes, he was a part of the protection ring. When the Mayor went to the next phase he gave Wulf the job of controlling the prostitution."

Now I want to ask the question that makes my heart beat fast like a piston. "What was Wulf's involvement with Charlie's murder?" I have to make sure the answer doesn't make me react.

While huffing he says, "He pulled the trigger."

I keep everything in check when I ask my follow up. "Did you take the picture?"

He bows his head down as he says a somber, "yes."

I start gritting my teeth and clenching my jaw. I think I bit the inside of my lip I now taste irony blood.

"You had gotten too close. It made the Mayor nervous. He wanted to make you into an example for anyone who thought they wanted out. When you left the force he kept tabs on you. When you started renting that office he decided to start another of his relocation programs in that neighborhood."

"What's the relocation program?" I asked feeling uninformed.

"He has me buy buildings with his money putting my name on the deeds. He takes a neighborhood that is up and coming or trendy. He gets the death squad who have the sway on drugs, gambling, and prostitution and introduces them in."

"The property value goes down and he will eventually pull them out and send in the cops. Then make a big profit. He plans on doing that in two years."

That's when his final term ends. I ask already knowing the answer, "did you kill that old man who owned my building before you goose stepped your way in?"

With his head still lowered he answers a quiet almost regretful, "yes."

I do what I do best and ignore this revelation and keep going. "He got to kill two birds, watch me and buy up the real estate. This thing with Herodes, the Mayor wanted to be some real estate mogul by blackmailing a real one into helping start a monopoly?"

"Yes, he feels his plan is taking too long. Owning drug dens and low income housing isn't placing him within the elite circle."

'Elite,' I confusingly think to myself, 'he's the fucking Mayor!' I can't say this; I have to keep the mood a serious tone. Instead I ask, "What's his endgame? So he becomes a real estate mogul, then what?" He doesn't seem like the type of man who will just stop at that.

"The Mayor confided to me that his dream is to own a multi-million dollar producing movie studio." He says.

I quickly turn away from his lowered head. Putting my hand over my mouth I hold in my laughter as much as I can without letting him see. My face turns red as I try to get in some calming breaths before turning my head back around. How fucking ridiculous.

What a convoluted plan just to achieve something so silly. Gotta have dreams I guess. I wish I could express how stupid I think this all is but don't want to spoil the Charles Bronson impression I'm doing here.

This jabroni just wants a position of power. Every time he does he's never satisfied and looks up to getting a better one. This guy is like a tick that never gets full. This interrogation has brought a wide variety of emotions from me.

Time to ask an important question, "Did the Mayor have Herodes killed?"

He doesn't answer at first. Then with his head still down he eventually answers. He doesn't hold anything back anymore. I definitely did a good job of breaking him. "Yes, he wouldn't budge with helping the Mayor. He had Rondo take him."

"While he was walking the dog?"

"Yes," he says. "The Mayor gave him another chance after that but Rondo had hit him too hard. He was already too far gone. The Mayor was pissed, had Rondo dump the body in the river. Then had the cops cover up the investigation. He influenced them to declare Herodes dead quicker than they normally would."

That's what I already gathered. I'm contemplating whether I should tell the kid.

Time to switch gears. "We've gone over the Mayor's master plan. Now give me a list on the inner circle within the death squad and what they're in charge of."

He spits out blood onto his floor. He wheezes, coughs, and then speaks. "Out of the ten, five of us act like his 'generals'. We're the ones in charge of the five activities that make money." 'Activities' I like that, like their camp counselors.

"Wulf is in charge of prostitution which lead to brothels. Hill deals with the gun running." That is some hardcore shit right there. "Harris regulates the gangs, and Mendes handles the underground gambling."

"Now gambling's involved? The fat man has a lot of fingers in pies." I say in a non-jokey way. "What about drugs, you forgot about drugs, wasn't that your partner?"

With his head still down he says, "Did I?" This comes out in a mischievous way. Almost as if he purposely left out the fifth name. He picks his head up to look at me. "My partner or my ex-partner's name is Victor Ramirez."

'Ok, so what, that doesn't mean anything to me. That build up seemed pointless' I'm thinking.

"You may know him as, Hermano De Sangre." This is the moment that if I was drinking something I would spit it out from sheer shock.

"Blood? That fucking loon was a cop?" What a strange piece to an already absurd puzzle. It also dawns on me I once asked this asshole if he knew that other asshole. That means this asshole lied to me. Although he did a convincing job of lying I must give him a harder whack next time.

"When the Mayor gave him the position of running the drug distribution, it eventually went to his head. He quit the force and became a self-pointed drug lord. Now he's starting a war with the Mayor."

Then I remember, one of Blood's henchmen had talked about a 'puppet master'. Jesus, I guess that shitty song is right, it is a small world. Everything is connected and it leaves a bad taste in mouth. I have fallen into a crazy web filled with crazy people. It's sad when I can pass for the normal one.

My shock in this recent revelation almost makes me forget a question involving Blood's whereabouts. "Is Blood's' lair' in the same place?" I almost cringe saying that word. I ask remembering when I was last there and I escaped. He would have moved if he had any brains and the jury is still out on that.

He picks his head up, "I don't know. He always manages to stay well hidden."

"You mean to tell me you don't have any detail on where your ex-partner currently operates out of? Not to mention your boss's sworn enemy." I call bullshit. I could always try the original spot if I had time.

"We found out they deal near the corner of sixty-second avenue and Kirby Street. In your neighborhood. They use an ice cream truck to supply the drugs. It's also stocked with ice cream." Whew, for a second there I was worried no one would be able to get their Choco Taco's.

Ice cream trucks as cover? What movie did they take that from, because I know that is not an original concept.

I get some ideas. This looks like a better idea than walking into a creepy warehouse unannounced. I look down at him and say "you've been a good host but I need a few things from you before I go."

I grab his wallet which I already took out of his pants when he was knocked out. I take all his money out, he's got close to three-hundred in here, hutch money bitch! He doesn't react or resist, he puts his head back down to sulk in his pain.

Next I ask him, "Does the Mayor live in Kalani?" I'm thinking the same place that Herodes called home.

"Yes, on top of the hill." I knew it and big surprise it's the biggest house in the richest neighborhood. On top of one of the highest points in the city. To look over his empire of shit. Also, this guy wants to be even richer? What does he want a palace in the sky?

"One last thing you're going to do for me," I say to him. "You're going to sign over the deed of my building to me."

His head stays down. He doesn't say anything.

I smack him in the back of the head. "I can't do that!" He looks up at me. "The mayor will kill me."

I take my blade out. I place it by his testicle area over his pants. "If you don't do this, I won't kill you, I will just turn you into a eunuch. That would be far worse. A big man like you, those three little things in your pants are your best friends." I say in a flat voice.

Damn, look at me I'm a fucking psycho! It seems to work though because that spot where I have my blade, it starts to get wet. That dampness gets larger. For a guy who has been bullying me around since he bought the building he sure is acting like a huge pussy right now. Funny how a little pain will turn into fear. I wouldn't know.

"Ok, ok, I'll do it. Just don't castrate me." I move the knife away. "But it's going to take me a few days, I'll have to get a lawyer. The Mayor can't find out."

"He won't and you will get your few days. Don't fuck me on this or I'm going to collect your balls." I contemplated killing him for his part in Charlie's murder but he's better to me alive for now. Besides I know I just sentenced him to a fate worse than death.

When Fatty Arbuckle and the other cops find out what he did, and they will find out, good old Powers is going to wish I killed him. I just hope that comes after he signs the deed over to me.

I untie him and he assures me he plans on doing what I ask. "I'd like to give you some advice before I go, it was passed on to me by a wise man." I say sarcastically without changing my tone.

I lean in close and whisper into his ear. "Power is not found in guns, fists, or even money. It's information that topples governments. Its secrets that keep people in line." I pull back from his ear hiding my smirk. "You remember that."

I go back to my office. It's been a busy and intense morning. I look at my right hand and it's red and raw like hamburger meat from the beating I gave Powers. By the way, everything I did back there I learned from the Captain Thunder training book I have. From the choke hold to how to break a finger. Yeah, that's an intense book.

I couldn't care much for the 'training' I learned when I was a faceless man. Most of that got flushed away. Especially since the Captain Thunder book taught me most of that years prior. That book has not steered me wrong.

I relax by throwing back a cold one or five. This has been a long journey. I can't say it's been a happy one.

When did my life become so complicated? I miss the old days when I would drink, do the occasional easy job involving lollipops, drink, and find myself in hilarious situations. That last one never happened.

Anyway, can't complain, it is what it is. I curse myself for saying that, I hate that phrase. Only people who can't admit when a situation sucks say that. As my head starts to get light headed I start to zone thinking about boss Hogg.

I still have that tape and I have to use it against him especially for Astra's sake. Then before I go to the blackouts, before my brain stops being useless to me I come up with an idea, two actually.

Before I execute either one I first have to run an errand of most importance and it's a secret. I will then go to Kalani. All the way to the top. Luckily I know a certain security guard that can hook me up, for seventy-five dollars. Not to mention the cab it cost to get here.

I have Powers to thank for enough ample bread to afford that. Then I'll go implement the second plan.

I feel the blackouts creep up on me. Despite coming up with a great plan. It's because I made my brain work so hard during intoxication to come up with such a great plan. That now I have no energy to fight them off. So I guess I'm going to have execute both ideas tomorrow as I once again slip off into unconsciousness.

11

I wake up as tomorrow never comes. I think breaking Powers and the combination of the hutch just created a power nap. I feel awake, alert, and a little drunk. Sounds like a good idea to start the plans. I just hope it's not too late to do the first part.

Turns out it wasn't and now it's time to head up to Kalani. At my first stop I decide to pay a certain little girl that doesn't totally get on my nerves a visit. I get to the gate of her house, press the button and after a second the gate opens.

Astra comes running out with her arms open. "Mister, mister you came back!" She hugs me as I stand there uncomfortable.

All I can do is pat her back, "yeah, hey, how's it going?" Almost immediately following her is the dog, Piddles, still a dumb name.

She gets off me. "What are you doing here mister, to see me?"

"No," I respond almost instantly. "I came to see a friend," I use that word very loosely. I notice that by saying I wasn't here to see her and that basically she wasn't a friend caused her to bow her head in sadness.

I quickly try to rectify the situation. "Oh, and to see you of course, my buddy." I say this and pat her on the back awkwardly. It gets her to smile nevertheless.

"So, how's it going?" What am I supposed to say, 'sorry your dad's dead'? I don't know what I'm doing here. Maybe I care, maybe I don't. Or maybe I care just enough to feel a little bad about her dad that I wanted to see if she was ok.

"Mister?" She asks completely ignoring my weak attempt to try to connect. "Is my daddy in heaven with mommy?"

Jeez, I'm glad I came. I try my best to confront her. "Maybe?" Ugh, must do better. "Look hunny wherever he is he loves you, he misses you, and he'll always be with you as long as you remember him in your heart. The same goes for mommy." Wow, who's that guy? He's much better than that smelly drunk.

She says, "thanks mister," as she puts her little arms around me again and hugs.

This is a sweet moment, something I don't have often, sometimes by choice. If I have to admit I'm glad, I could help in any small way. I respond to her sweet gesture by patting her on the back.

We say our goodbyes, she watches me leave and waves as the dog runs around her and barks. She told me Mr. Black is taking care of her. That would make me feel better, if I cared, because you know I don't. I don't believe me either.

After a lengthy walk uphill I make it to the Mayor's mansion. The sun is just about to hide amongst the horizon as I ring the bell to his gate. If Herodes house was a mansion this place looked more like a fortress. With all the cameras and security, you would think he was Pablo Escobar rather than a public official.

A voice from the front gate speaker asks what do I want. When I tell them I have the tape the gate opens immediately.

A few minutes later I'm the Mayor's office. Marble floors, oak desk double the length and size of the fat man, and floor to ceiling glass windows behind him. So he can gaze upon the entire city, his growing empire. What a crock of shit.

I throw the mini recordable audio tape on his desk as he sits behind it smoking a Cuban. With Rondo lurking right behind him. How do I know it's a Cuban? Because it looks like a commie, I don't know I'm just guessing it's the best for this lardass.

"Youse made da right decision son." He says in his perfect English as he takes the tape and holds it in his fat sausage fingers hand.

"This ensures the safety of Astra and anyone else unlucky enough to be a part of this fucked up situation?"

"Dat's right son, you have my word." Which means absolutely dick to me. He goes on to say, "I didn't know youse cared son."

"I don't care. I just don't want to be responsible for anyone again." Or feel guilty.

"Sure son, sure." He half scoffs at my comment as he puffs from his phallic object.

"How much money did it cost to light that thing? Do you use the whole bill to light it up or do you have a wad of singed hundred dollar bills? You know you don't have to prove you're an obnoxious wannabe kingpin by doing things like that. I already made that judgment the moment I met you."

He ignores me and just looks at his cigar as he blows out the smoke. "Youse know a cigar is a lot like a woman."

"No, not this shit again! That metaphor comparing a woman to a cigar crap, I've heard it already. You and Blood deserve each other." I realize I let my cards show a little. Not enough where he would figure out how I know.

His eyebrows raise a little as if to say 'how do youse know', but I try to deflect his suspicions. "Can we move this along, don't you have a tape to break in front of me so you can show your dominance or some shit?"

He puts his cigar in his mouth and smirks. "Have it youse way son." He clenches his hand into a hard fist while the tape is still inside. He opens his hand and smirks to reveal, that the tape is still intact.

He frowns upon his discovery, gets discouraged and tries again. This time he's sweating. Veins are popping out of his neck and temples.

I could only imagine this is what he looks like when he's on the bowl. Which after witnessing his typical diet I'm not surprised. He must shit out bricks.

He opens his hand confident in the knowledge that he's done it this time. Inside his already sweaty hand is the tape wholly intact. Now it's got some blood on it from him trying too hard.

I think this is hilarious but I try not to laugh. I do say with my face and tone in total serious mode, "those corners can be lethal." He grits his teeth and hands it behind him to Rondo who grabs the tape in one hand and crushes it in one try.

"Ok, we done here?" I turn around and start to leave his office.

He says to me as I'm trying to leave, "How's it feels to be a jellyfish?"

"Excuse me?" I ask already knowing damn well what he means.

"To go tru life without a backbone. Pretending youse don't care for anyones. Sulking around and brooding about youse loses. Youse no man, youse a jellyfish." Although I can't see his face I know he's smirking as he blows smoke out of his greasy pie hole.

I could walk away and leave it alone but I have to retort. Without turning I start talking. "I maybe a jellyfish but there is no earthy description for you. To call you a human is offensive to the human race.

You are lower than a person. Slime looks down on you."

I decide to hit below his man gunt. I turn around. "I change my mind. You are a far bigger man than I am and not just in weight. You have hopes and dreams. You are trying to make something out of yourself while I cruise through life mooching and wallowing in my pain."

"Or maybe, I don't care. Maybe I don't wallow. I numb myself by self-medicating, because I don't want to care. Maybe I'm not in a sense of self-pity."

"I know I have hurt people. There's nothing I can do about that. There's no one to blame but me. Maybe I'm more in a sense of self-aware. Maybe I'm realistic and I know how the world works. Maybe you shouldn't destroy audio tapes before listening to them."

Then I tilt my head down to look up at him and show off my devilish grin. "Good luck getting that movie studio you naïve fat fuck!"

Then I walk out of the room go down the stairs and out the front door. All the while the Mayor is screaming so loud I can still hear him at the front gate. He hasn't sent Rondo after me. He is probably in too much of shock and rage. I know that won't last.

I didn't give him the tape. That's where I stopped off at before coming here. I shouldn't have exposed that to him just yet. What can I say he pissed me off with that 'jellyfish' comment. I am going to continue using that anger to get the ball rolling on my second plan.

Let me make this clear though: I do not want to execute this idea. Although if I am going forward with my plan of revenge this must be done.

This plan will help insure the Mayor goes down. He is the first step before I can go after the rest of his death squad. Cut the head off the fat cobra and the rest should fall in line. Great theory that probably won't work.

I prepare myself mentally for the most mind numbing conversation that is about to take place. It's time to make alliances that I normally wouldn't even waste any time on making. These be desperate times.

The next step is to make arrangements to meet with my soon to be new 'partner'. That is if he agrees with my plan. In the next bunch of hours, I will hope to convince Hermano De Sangre with helping me take down the Mayor. This is what they call a cliffhanger.

PART III: THE FAT MAN SLEEPS

WITH THE SWEDISH FISHES

1

Champ's world is changing, whether he wants it to or not. To find any small amount of peace in his jumbled life, or 'hero' attempts to make a deal with one devil hoping to defeat another. Presenting what may be the final chapter in the existence of the prince of cynicism.

It's been a life changing six months. Don't get me wrong, I still drink as if my life depends on it and it does. No, I'm referring to the little tryst I've made with Hermano de Sangre. It was awkward for me to say the least. Flashback time!

The day after having that switcheroo pow wow with the Mayor I had set my sights on contacting Blood. The problem was, how was I going to do that? It's not like I have a douchebag signal handy that I could shoot into the sky.

I had gone back to his old 'lair' which had been emptied. This makes sense.

Then I vaguely remembered what Powers said about the ice cream truck distributing in my neighborhood. I try to pluck that memory from my hutch induced blob of a brain. Then it dawned on me it's supposed to be parked on sixty-second and Kirby Street.

There was a line at the truck when I got there. I ordered a Choco Taco and mentioned talking to Blood. After a few minutes arguing with the dealer of the highly addictive substance and the drugs, he finally gets in contact with someone.

I told the ice cream horse jockey I knew he was connected to Blood. Since I could see his DEAD tattoo on the inside of his upper right arm between his elbow and armpit.

After getting blindfolded again I arrive at his presumably new 'liar'. The ambiance was very reminiscent of a rerun of Lucha Libre mixed with Dark Shadows.

Blood is once again standing in the back by an altar with half melted candles on top of skulls. He turns around wearing a suit along with his painted up face. He then walks up to me. "Ah, if it isn't the man who shit's when in the presence of Hermano de Sangre," He says as he smirks.

"If it isn't the giant Mexican with the B.O. problem and the issue with differentiating reality." I say as his smirk fades.

"Look I didn't come here to trade love quips. We both have a common enemy, the Mayor." He stands there going from an angry look to now a blank confused look. I sigh and roll my eyes as I say, "the puppet master?"

He knows who I meant the first time. He's so stuck in this sick game of his it's more of an obsession he can't stop. He reminds me of a Batman villain.

With the sheer mention of the Mayor's pseudonym Blood starts to go apeshit. He rips his nice suit shirt without taking off his jacket in the process. "You do not speak of the puppet master in the presence of the Blood!!!"

"Alright, calm down Victor." I say which catches him off guard. He stops his little temper tantrum to shoot me a shockingly puzzled look on his face created by my nugget of truth.

The expression quickly fades as he looks away from me. That's when he says calmly "I'm surprised you didn't kill Simbudyal, Leonard." That wipes whatever smug look I had on my face and replaces it with utter shock.

I guess my name isn't as secretive as I thought. He just took my one comment that injected a bit of reality into his facade turned it around and then did the same thing to me.

Then it dawns on me that he was Powers, or Simbudyal's partner. Then he confirms my suspicion. "You're not the only one who was watching that house." He says in a completely normal voice.

Then it again dawns on me that he was there the night Charlie died. Before I could make a comment he starts to speak still looking away from me.

"I...am regretful about what happened...that night. You must know that I didn't have anything to do with..." He's talking about Tina, Charlie's wife. He trails off and doesn't finish the sentence but we both know where he was going with it. All I can do is nod.

He goes back to being an ass. "Hermano de Sangre will accept your invitation to join forces. Yes, the enemy of my enemy...is my friend." He says as he makes a fist and brings it up to his face and stares at it intensely. Then he just snaps out of it.

"Whatever plan you have; Hermano de Sangre will join you. Together we will eradicate the tyranny that plagues this city, from the," he yells this next part, "scourge that is known as the puppet master!!!"

"You do realize you're just a drug dealer right? You only want to 'eradicate him' so he doesn't bother you when you expand your business. Don't act like you're saving the city from him, aren't you just as bad?"

It didn't bother me that I had just insulted a hulking mass filled with rage who tower's over me by two feet. That's my lack of a filter conveniently acting up so why should it?

He turns around as I start to regret what I said. It turned out he was setting up for another tangent. "There is more to me than just a gain for territory or money. This is about a personal journey with self-discovery and revenge against that power hungry fat man."

"Whatever," I say as I roll my eyes. If I had lingered on my guilt or wallowed in my pity I think I would have turned into this schmuck, minus the face paint. I'm talking more like being overdramatic, schizophrenic, and stuck in the past. "Is there some easy way I can contact you?"

He automatically whistles, one of those loud high pitch whistles that doesn't require a hand to complete. Then a minion came out from the back and hands Blood a phone. He gave it to me and explained it's a burner phone with a contact number already programmed into it.

Then he said, "Do not mistake my kindness or this partnership as anything more than a necessity. When this is over, beware, for I am still to be treated as, deadly." He says emphasized on the word 'beware' and 'deadly'.

That was it, I took his stupid threat for the backstage WWE comment it was and I went on my merry way. A partnership built on a mutual hatred for the Mayor and for each other. What could go wrong? I told him I'd contact his as soon as I had a plan. That was half a year ago. I still have nothing in terms of 'a plan'.

They had a funeral for Herodes. The faceless men had deemed his case from a possible kidnapping to a possible homicide. Since they didn't have any evidence either way because the Mayor was covering it up. It quickly became a cold case.

The family however weren't convinced that he was dead so they held off performing a service for a while.

It became a huge event. All the big hitters were there, including his honor, which is such a dickhead move. The biggest star of the city also joined the festivities, me. Well, I only went to the burial.

Plus, I was far enough away from everyone so I wouldn't be asked things like, 'who are you' and 'why do you look like that?' I could see Astra; she was in tears the whole time. By the way for the record, I was not there because I cared, it was strictly for my ongoing case. That sounds like bullshit to me too.

That girl has been through a lot. On top of burying her father both sides of the rest of the family are fighting for custody. I'm not surprised that they could be at the funeral and act all cordial to each other. This fight of theirs is really for the kid's inheritance. That's just my 'the glass is never full' attitude.

While I was practically hiding in the bushes like a stalker the Fat Man minus Jake noticed me. He then sent Rondo to chase me off but I left before it could get to that.

Ever since Powers signed the apartment over, Fatty Arbuckle is just trying to keep his distance from me.

By the way that went without a problem. Just had to wait a few weeks for him to get a bent lawyer on board. I was surprised it wasn't a big issue. I must have really put the fear of God into Powers. If every encounter could be that easier. So I'm a landlord now. Let me tell you, it sucks.

I thought manipulating Powers into handing over the building to me would take some pressure off. Stupid move because all it did was make more.

Sure, I don't have to worry about rent but now I have to worry about collecting the rent. The first order of business was to kick out the drug dealers on the ground floor and surprisingly that wasn't much trouble either.

Apparently it has something to do with what happened with Powers. Turns out I have some street cred, eh, whatever, it will go away and I'll be treated like a leper again.

I guess Powers had created this persona for himself on the streets for being some sort of a tough guy. Hence why no one would ever dare shit on his car. Although as we all found out this wasn't true.

The beating and getting him to give me this place hit the streets. It then gained me respect if you could believe that. It's like prison rules. People have stopped seeing me as a punk. Well maybe I'm not that high on the totem pole. I'm above punk but below rockface. Yeah, I was that far down originally.

Powers on the other hand, fell from grace much further than I rose. He's below punk and just above snitch. He lost his spot on the Slug's death squad. I still don't know who replaced him it yet. I do know he's become a joke at his job, bullied even.

I wouldn't be surprised if he quits or dies. Don't you dare feel bad for him? I have a certain picture that requires me to never feel bad for that asshole. Just thinking about this has turned me into a potty mouth.

By the way can we talk about what kind of street totem pole categorizes punk above rockface? Someone will have to explain it to me eventually. I'll never understand the streets.

In any case, getting those drug addicts out of the first floor was just the first step. The next was finding someone to fill in the vacant apartments.

Plus, I had no idea there was another living spot on the first floor. It's towards the back of the floor, underneath the staircase. I've been here for a few years and never noticed. No one ever said I was a good Marlowe.

Eventually I was able to get someone in the first apartment. The new tenants are a couple of stoners. So I went up a level from mean, violent drug dealers to slow, passive, borderline retarded pot smokers.

The next step I have to do if I want to turn this place into a money maker is renovate the aforementioned first floor apartment. Also the other one on my floor, and the two on the third floor. They've all been abandoned for a while and that's why I never mentioned them.

What cash am I using to get all this work done you ask? Very astute of you by the way. When Powers signed over this place he added a bit of a 'signing bonus' in the total of fifty thousand. Making it a bit of a thank you for taking this garbage heap off his hands.

Not much of a big surprise to say the least, it was my idea. He had a lot saved up. Hey, torture and breaking someone's fingers can go a long way. That's how the mob stayed in business for so long.

This recent spike in income has opened me up a bit. To do things I wouldn't do normally like renovate a whole building. It also equals out to a lot of drinking. Honestly though it hasn't opened me up that much, I still have bouts of chronic boredom. I just want to quit like every time I try.

My mind wanders into getting a better lock for my door. More to put on the to do list that I don't want to do.

I was lucky that the whole deal I made with Powers or how it transpired didn't become common knowledge until he signed it over to me. I had tried hard to keep it from everyone beforehand, especially the Mayor. Then when it went through Fatty had it out for me.

He knows I gave him an empty audio tape. Frankly I don't care. I'm trying to get him so angry he focuses that wrath on me. It can also backfire on me and he'll go after Astra or even worse, Sarah. That's why I'll have to come up with something soon.

Just imagining his face getting all red and sweaty at the fact that I fucked him over does makes me smile. It's the little things in life that make it worth wild. Well that and drinking.

Speaking of Sarah, I've talked to her here and there. That's how I got the info on Powers current situation becoming a Peter Parker. The loser who gets bullied, not the super strong man spider.

I think she hates me less but doesn't completely forgive me. The only way that would happen is if I tell her the whole truth. How I was responsible for that thing I feel responsible for. That's not going to happen for a while though. I can't even say what happened out loud, alone.

Well, you're all caught up now. I've had a busy schedule. The three empty apartments need to get painted, the furnace has to get looked at, may need a new one. All the windows need to get replaced, and there's no toilet in any of the apartments on the third floor. No toilet at all! Talk about crapping on the go.

With all these objectives I have to do I think the best thing to do first is, drink and sleep! Exposition gets me thirsty and tired.

2

I wake up energized, refreshed, and thirsty. Even though I went to bed drunk enough to be exposed to the blackouts. My body would prefer to get some hutch in me before the good mood I'm experiencing gets ruined with thoughts of responsibility.

When I leave my building I am greeted by a full moon. Surprised upon seeing the bright round face because I did not realize it was night time.

I'm walking to the Kamikaze bar. It's a bit of a distance from my building. It's in a way better neighborhood.

Most of the bars aren't filled with cheap booze and O.D.ing patrons. The crowd there is also much more diverse. Compared to the lousy alcoholics like me, wasted druggies, or rowdy frat boys. The other groups I'm used to drinking with.

While I'm on my way there I can't help but let my mind wander. Whenever I get a moment to myself it's always spent with my brain somewhere else. This time it's on my money situation.

Once my 'trust fund' runs out, I'll have to start looking for jobs again, ugh. Because I know the rent flowing in will not be enough for my crazy lifestyle. Unless I can get all the rent from the five apartments coming in. That's if and only if I can get respectable, reputable tenants.

Trying to gentrify a whole neighborhood single handedly is exhausting and a bit dehydrating.

After finishing those depressing thoughts I turn them to the bar I'm heading to. The Kamikaze is one of those themed bars. I think the offbeat theme is what makes it popular.

The whole place is made to look like a WWII Japanese fighter plane. The outside of the bar has a giant propeller coming out of the wall that looms all the way to the ground.

Inside is plastered with pictures of Japanese pilots and aerial shots of flying planes. The propeller from outside connects with a fighter plane constructed inside and hung from the ceiling.

I turn the corner that will ultimately lead me straight to the bar. That's literally four blocks straight till I get there. As soon as I made that left on Byrne Ave I noticed the flashing lights in the distance. They belonged to the faceless men. When I get half a block closer to them I realized they are surrounding the Kamikaze.

I keep walking because now I'm curious. Also I'm a bit pissed that someone ruined what would have been fun drinking night with causing a little trouble mixed in.

I get to the block before the bar and there are at least four cop cars including one of their special unit trucks. The whole block the bar is on is taped off. This leaves the huge crowd of gawkers to stand in the street which also extends to the block across from the bar.

Now normally I would stay away anything the faceless men are involved in. However, like I said I'm curious and pissed. I'm more self-aware of just how much I can get away with since acquiring the building.

That little bit of street cred helps since that's pooled over into the faceless men world too. I'm known as the guy who kicked the great Derek Powers ass. That actually means something to these donut dunkers.

I start in the back of the crowd. I slowly move my way inside until I'm in the front. "Champ, hey man." I'm behind the yellow tape watching all these so called 'police officers' standing around and doing nothing. "Hey Champ, dude." They keep coming in and out of the bar.

"Dude!" I am in the best angle to see the inside of the bar every time they open the front door. "Champ, like over here." When the door fly's open for the first time the situation is just a small puzzle piece.

"Hey man, over here." Every time it swings open and close the more and more pieces get added until I can comprehend what's going on. The finished result is blood, a lot of blood.

I turn my head to the right and see three white guys with dreads. One of them has been trying to get my attention for a minute. I turn it back around because you never pay attention to white guys with dreads. Do you know how dirty their hair has to be until it can be considered a dread? That's all it is, dirty fucking hair.

Dreads on white guys usually equals druggie losers. Dreads on white women usually means druggie sluts.

When I turned from quickly looking I got a glimpse of one of them. It eventually registered in my head that they looked familiar. In doing so it caused me to stop in mid turn and then go back to look at the three. The middle one starts waving his hands in the air. "Hey man!"

I don't react, because I don't know him.

"What's going on dude, like you see this shit?" he comes closer to me. His eyes are barely open as if he just came out of a Cheech and Chong marathon. He's got a big dumb smile on his face like he ate the best burrito ever.

I give him a look on my face that says I'm trying to think of who you are but it's not working. Either that or I'm shitting myself.

He understands it's not the expression where I would need a

change of underwear. "It's Roach man!"

I still have this look on my face but I now know full well who this is. It's my tenant who lives on the first floor. Real name is Chester, saw it on his I.D. when he got the apartment.

I did a pretty thorough check on him, Sarah helped. He comes from money, big into pot, wants to live the bohemian lifestyle I guess. He seems like a nice kid albeit a dope.

"Hey Chester." As soon as I gleefully say this his face scrunches up since he doesn't want his friends to hear his embarrassing name. Now I can understand that but instead of wanting to relate or bond with him, I'd rather cause trouble. Especially since I was denied doing so in my bar of choice.

"No like its Roach dude," he says as he turns his head to make sure his friends aren't in ear shot. As he does I smirk to myself. Roach, that's the kind of name twelve-year olds who think their cool give themselves.

His friends, who I think are his roommates get closer as Chester starts changing the subject about his name. I say 'I think' because I cannot be bothered with knowing them.

Before he can talk I interrupt him. "What are you doing here? Don't you have a hacky sack tournament somewhere?" I ask as a joke but say it deadpan to be a dick.

"Don't be fucked up bro." He says with a serious look despite the red eyed high look he has. "That's tomorrow." Of course it is I think, my attempt at a joke becomes a reality and I am not surprised.

"What happened here?" I asked in my most curious tone acting like a real Marlowe. My need to know all things mysterious comes out.

"Dude that shit was like crazy!" He says going back to his shit eating grin and his eyes are too heavy look. "This guy walked into the bar."

"What is this, the beginning of a fucking joke?" I ask.

Tweedle dee and Tweedle dumb are now standing on either side of him. Zippy the pinhead on his right starts to open his yap. "No dude, this isn't like a joke or anything." You could put these three in a lineup and I would have real trouble picking them out. Their so similar they even take jokes literal the same way.

"Fine, just tell me what the fuck happened?"

The third Muske-dumbass starts talking. "So like this guy walks into the bar." Didn't we establish this? From worry of starting a 'Who's on First' routine I don't say this out loud. "He walks up at the end of the bar and buys a pint of beer."

"Yeah, but it was like the way he looked when he ordered it." The guy on Chester's right says. "He was wearing one of those shirts with bright colors and flowers on them, what are they called?" He asks the other two who don't know what he's talking about.

"A Hawaiian shirt?" I ask. Fucking dumbasses.

"Yeah, I remember thinking who wears those?" Maybe Hawaiians I think to myself. I sometimes know when to keep my mouth shut. "He also had like this huge smile on his face as he looked around. I thought that was, like odd." So says the grown white man with dreads and hemp shorts.

"Yeah and it wasn't the kind of smile that shows teeth. Just a grin. I noticed it cause I thought it looked odd and creepy. Then he starts randomly talking to the guy that was standing next to him at the bar. But like the guy doesn't pay him, like any attention," says Chester. "He just turns to like drink his beer."

"Yeah but like the whole time still smiling wide. And he drinks that shit in one shot." The left one said.

"Yeah and he just wipes his mouth with his arm when he's done like it's nothing." The right one says, at least I think it's the right one.

At this point their all interrupting and talking over each other I start to lose track of who's talking. Their all one person anyway. What's with the 'likes' by the way? When did this generation all speak as if they were valley girls? I realize I'm not that much older but this choice of language makes me feel, well like, an old coot.

I am very interested in this story even though it's getting mangled by Huey, Dewey, and Louie. "When he's done drinking he like looks at the empty mug with that smile." I've quit trying to keep track with who said what.

"Yeah, then he takes the empty pint and smashes it into the guy next to him. Right in the back of his head. You know, the one who ignored him. It was like so strange he didn't look mad when he ignored him or when he hit him with the glass. Just always with that smile."

"The guy's friends helped him. No one noticed the smiling guy so they ignored him."

"Yeah but like the bartender did so he goes over to the smiling guy. And like he says something to him."

"Yeah, I heard it even over the noise, he like said his name I guess. Then he said 'did I ever tell you why they call me Happy'. Then he takes the jagged part of the broken glass and jams it into the bartender's neck."

"Yeah, like it was fucking crazy. Blood spurted everywhere. People were screaming."

"Then like the bouncer came over. This guy was still holding the jagged beer pint but he dropped it and hit the big bouncer in the throat. He like karate chopped him in the jugular!"

"Yeah and like people were screaming and started running out of the place. Some were on their cellphones calling the cops. I'm pretty sure they were trying to take pictures. Shit I did but it was too dark and far away."

I forgot which one showed me his attempt at getting a shot. It was too dark. They go back to gleefully telling their story. Like a kid jumping around eager to tell his parents what happened in school that day.

"When we ran out the guy was still smiling but not wide eyed crazy smiling. No, just smiling like in a senior picture. He had walked around the bar and was touching the bartender who looked like he was dying. Other bouncers started running towards him."

"Yeah and like that's all we saw." One of them said. After they looked at me again as children awaiting for praise from their father.

"What did he look like, other than what he was wearing?"

"Oh man, he was not tall, but like not short," one said.

"Yeah and not fat, but not skinny either. Kinda muscly, but not jacked, you know?" The other idiot said.

"Dude, he was blond though, like, what's it called, not silver," he thinks hard I could almost see the smoke coming out of his ears. Then he snaps his fingers and says, "Platinum, his hair was platinum blond." He said as he smiled and kept his eyes at half-staff.

"One more thing, why were you here? This place doesn't really seem like your thing." So says the guy who refers to himself as a loner barfly.

"Well," Chester started to say, "Sometimes you need something a little different in your hangout spot." I hate knowing we came up with similar ideas. "Spending almost every night smoking weed in our place can like, get boring, you know?"

I get an idea to spice up this disappointing situation. "So you mean to tell me that you're explaining to an ex-cop and your current landlord, that you smoke marijuana in <u>my</u> apartment!?"

The three of them start to get nervous by sweating and stammering, all at once. "Uh, no, you see, the thing is, like, well, uhhhhh." That was Moe (Chester).

"Hey man, you got it all wrong, he was just like, uh, he, uh, meant the last apartment, yeah." That was Larry (the left one).

"Dude, he's on to us, fucking run!!!" That was Shemp (the right one), he's not worthy enough to be called Curly.

They start running and bumping into people in the crowd who are yelling at them. I can only stand there and smile. Where are they running to, I know where they live. A worthy attempt at salvaging a once good mood turned into a crummy night.

I leave this circus and walk to a nearby bar that I've never been to before. It's your typical craphole. I sit over my mixed drink made from cheap liquor disappointed over my spoiled night.

I reflect on how I hate when things don't go according to plan. That's what makes me an adult baby. I can't but think about this blond Hawaiian shirt wearing smiling jackass. Seemed too random to be a random act of violence.

Of all the people in the bar why the beer jockey? I mean, the three amigos probably deserve to die more. No, that's not right. I didn't even know the bartender, maybe he did deserve it.

These are more W&H questions that I file away that will probably never get answered. So I drink drowning my disappointments until the blackouts come. I would have liked drinking under a WW2 fighter plane.

3

I wake up on my back. I open my eyes to see a concrete slab a few inches from my face. Confused I yawn and try to crawl my way out. As I slowly creep to my left I start to think there is no way out of this stone coffin.

Then I notice there is no more floor to shuffle to. It goes straight down to the river. I'm under a fucking bridge like a fucking troll!

Being completely clueless on how I got here I shimmy my way out. Careful I don't fall into the sludge poorly called our reservoir. Immediately afterwards I stand up and dust myself off.

Turns out I was somehow wedged in the crawl space between the Morrison Bridge and the column that goes into the water. I climb up a service ladder and get onto the street.

Another fine mess I've gotten myself into. I could say that was the strangest place I ever woke up from but I'd be lying. Wait...no, no I'd be lying. Not being anywhere near a bus I take a long time to get back to my place.

The long trek home has made me thirsty and tired. Guess which one I do first? As I suck on the Mother's milk that is my liquor bottle I can't help but contemplate about the Mayor. It's mainly about how the hell am I going get Blood and his highness together?

This becomes a two-day event trying to come up with a plan. Sitting and drinking, dinking and sitting, with sleeping sprinkled in between.

The best thing I can come up with is getting Blood's army to storm the Mayor's castle. If I do that the faceless men will be up in our grill. Unless, I can convince the one person who has so far been absent from this circus to help.

He should have enough clout to head off the faceless men. In case you're still paying attention to this ramble I mean the Commissioner.

Commissioner Chyre is an older guy in his fifties, shorter, got a bit of weight on him. He looks like Teddy Roosevelt but gruffer. Past his old man glasses he's still grizzled looking.

He looks like he's seen a lot of shit in his day. Before being the Commish, a nickname he hates, he was a super cop. Being a hero a few times can get you a big promotion. Especially when a candidate for Mayor is struggling in the poles mainly due to his accusations of fraud and being a thief. That's when you need a little heroic boost.

I'm surprised a no nonsense guy like the Commish would hook up with a degenerate like the Mayor. When I was a faceless man and I was investigating the dirty ones, the Commish was the first one I looked into. Thinking he was behind it all, but he turned out to be clean.

I hate to admit but I looked up to the guy. Especially when I was in the academy, I strived to be a stand-up cop like him. Maybe I still do despite the cold, cynical, uncaring prick I've become.

He represents a constant reliable source stuck in the middle of this filthy, corrupt, letdown shit stain of a city. I ignore the sensible part of my brain that says he might be just as bad as the Mayor. Especially if he's been hooked up with him for this long.

I'll try to convince him to help and maybe find out why he's been in bed with that lardass. The notion that I've been very active lately hasn't escaped me. It starts to make me sick.

Snapping out of it I'm attempting to figure out how I am going to contact the Commish I get a spark of an idea in my brain. My new partner in crime Brother Blood was a cop. He may know something. I wanted to run my bum rush the Mayor's house idea by him regardless. I'm sure whatever answer he gives it's going to be yelled at me.

I use the burner phone I was given and when I hear the line get picked up I say "get me the Commissioner!"

The guy on the other line has no idea what I am talking about. I eventually get serious and tell him I want to see Blood. They pick me up and I go through the same spiel, blindfolded, secret location, candles, broody mood, and over acting. Let's get this over with.

"I have not heard from you in quite a while. I thought our partnership had dissolved. Maybe you had turned your back on the Blood!" he refers to himself in the third person while yelling with his back to me and his hands folded behind him.

"I finally had a plan getting the Mayor."

He quickly turns around; you can almost hear the whoosh. "The Blood is listening." Jeez, I had to associate myself with this lunk.

I let the idea rip. "We storm his mansion. We get your army and we show him what it means to mess with the Blood. It will be like D-day." I am really playing into his ego.

The idea is to let these two idiots hash it out as I'm in the back with the best seat in the house. Fuck it, maybe I'll steal something from the blob's house while I'm at it. He owes me that much.

Let's see if the big meathead takes to it. "This plan is most excellent! We shall rise from the tyrannical grip of the titiritero to storm his front door. We will chant loud and proud, 'we will not stand here and succumb to your opposing force. We will fight back and if you defeat us, we will emerge from the ashes to strike again'"!!!

His speech has taken a little wind out of him. He stands there huffing and puffing with a crazy look on his face.

"Will you calm the hell down?" I say annoyed at his antics. "You have to lay off the roids bro. That shit is going to give you a heart attack."

He stops breathing heavy. "Hermano de Sangre uses no such thing. Hermano de Sangre is driven by his own self-worth."

"That sounds about right. Look, for our plan to work we need the cops held back that night. If the Mayor calls in his personal guard, I figure you can handle that. With the whole force at his beck and call however, that might be a bit more than we can chew."

"Nothing is difficult with Blood's el ejército de los muertos!! But Hermano de Sangre does understand your point."

I shake my head. I don't try to hold back my contempt for his ridiculous behavior. Not that he even notices he's so swept up in his one-man play. "To figure out how we're going to keep the pigs at bay I need some info first."

He starts to open his mouth but before words can come yelling out and his arms start to flail I cut him off. "Just listen, the only way we can get to the force before the Mayor is if we contact the Commissioner."

Because he has to react to everything I say he starts to rev up his mouth box again. I go to interrupt him once more but this time he catches on and intercepts it.

"El Comisionado! That is a very bold idea. One that the Blood did not come up with himself. You show promise, one day you will be a lord who will command thousands with nothing but your voice."

"What the fuck does that shit mean? There's this exchange that people go through maybe you never learned. It's consists of asking you a question and you do this thing where you fucking answer it. Without giving a long winded monologue!" I lose my shit and screamed that last sentence.

He just stares at me with his brow wrinkled. The he starts to speak. "You have gained my respect. This partnership has blossomed into a friendship. You are my Hermano now." He lives in a dream world. "We are similar, you and I." If this fucking loon starts talking about his 'humble beginnings' I am going to puke on him.

"When I was a little boy growing up in the jungles of Mexico, I-"

"No," I loudly cut him off. "You are full of so much shit; you were born on the upper west side of the city."

His bravado gets dialed down a notch. "Yes, but I moved to Mexico when I was very little and-"

"No," I do it again. "You grew up here, you graduated from Midtown High. You were a cop; you went to fucking college your dingus!"

When he starts to talk his voice is more of a normal tone and he starts to look down like a little kid who got caught in a lie. "Yeah but, my father would take me there in the summers, reaping the fruits of-"

"No," I yell as I grow more and more annoyed. "Your father was Honduran and your mother was Mexican. You even have German and English descendants from your father's side. Any more lies you want me to clear up? I learned a lot of neat stuff about you." All thanks to Sarah, my ace in the hole.

His brow makes a frown again, this time a scrunched up set of lips join in. This makes a sad face as he looks down at the ground. "Stop playing a character Victor."

I say this more for my benefit than his. I'm fed up of talking to a delusional person, like a bored housewife who doesn't know that the soaps she watches aren't real. "Can you just talk like you're not an American Gladiator? We're alone, just between us, pass for something that's close to normal."

He keeps looking at the floor. Then he raises his head up and those stupid red contacts stare at me when he says, "alright."

He finally drops the WWE/Ricardo Montalban accent. His voice and tone become normal. You can tell it's very painful for him to do this. "Not in front of anyone, it's the only way I can keep them in line," he adds.

"Fine," I say as I roll my eyes. Then it dawns on me, "wait a minute, what about that Bond tech you have, the chip on the back of their neck shit? Isn't that how you keep them in line? Where did you get that stuff by the way?"

"Det. Hill, he works in Vice, my old department. He's in charge of the gun running. It's the most profitable for the Mayor, next to the drugs. My contacts with the drugs and the gangs, they got him into distributing the guns between gangs."

"Then he moved on to bigger clients, bigger mobs, than it became international. With that he was involved with heavier artillery. Currently his biggest supplier is the Russians."

That figures, it's always the Russians in the movies. Someone has to tell the Russians this isn't the movies and they should go back to being drunks and eating bear.

"They came up with the chip technology to keep their solders in line. I now use it for the same thing.

Hill and I have been working together secretly behind the Mayor. He's been providing me with hardware, I have been providing him with muscle. He will help us with Operation: Humpty Dumpty had a great fall."

Even when he's talking normal he still can't help but being an over dramatic prick. "Wait, this plan has an Operation name all of a sudden? You just can't help yourself, you have a sickness."

He ignores me, "when this is all done and we both get our revenge on the Mayor, I will help you get Wulf. I never liked him."

"Don't think you can butter me up. We are not friends," I tell him. "Now I need to know how I can get in contact with the Commish."

"I never had direct contact with him. But since I separated with the Mayor I tried to recon as much info on his allies as I could. I know where the Commissioner lives. I also know the Mayor has a very tight hold on him. Since he has no real say on what the Mayor does with his police force."

"You mean the mayor has some sort of dirt on the Commish?" I ask.

"So it would seem," he replies.

"Alright, let me get that address."

"I'll do you one better." He says as he moves his lips to whistle. Out comes a follower.

That's when Blood's back straightens and his chest pops back out. He goes back to speaking in a way where his sentences end in yelling.

"Blood is gracious enough to allow one of his most trusted. He will escort you to the next step in Operation: Humpty Dumpty had a great fall!" Jesus Christ what a rockface.

We leave. I follow the homicidal groupie as Blood is left by himself with his maniacal laughing. We enter into the same van that I have been kidnapped in so many times now. It's the first time I'm in the passenger seat, it feels weird, almost unnatural.

I start to make that noise one makes when you realize your mouth is dry, that almost clicking noise. All this convoluted storytelling is making me thirsty.

One can only hope that the Commish might have something at his place. That thought keeps me going.

The ennui that's always lurking in the pit of my stomach is slowly crawling and climbing its way to my brain.

I get bored easily and without hutch I start to get fidgety. Added to the fact that the brainless zombie driving me is in complete silence only makes my boredom increase. I get a nagging feeling that I might be tired. So I let that succumb over me. My eyes become heavy as I gladly slip into unconsciousness.

4

As I sleep I dream. It's not the same nightmare I have when I go to bed without drinking. This one is different I think because it's not a very deep sleep or a long one for that matter. I'm thinking about the first time, and the only time until today, that I met the Commissioner.

It was when I graduated the academy. He was handing out all the newly graduated their certificates. He had just become the Commish.

I remember the look on his face when he shook my hand after giving me my glorified piece of paper. He had a big smile under his caterpillar moustache. His eyes were filled with hope and pride. His handshake was firm and strong.

I knew who he was before that day. He was already known as the hero cop. I had looked up to him before I met him. Afterwards I was embarrassed when I started to think of him as more than a hero, but as someone I wish was my father.

I wake up from my little reminiscing dream when the van stops. We are an hour away from the city, in the middle of the woodsy mountains.

There is a gated wooden house. This must be the Commish's place. It looks like a small wood cabin. Until it kept getting more added to it. Then it became an extravagant two story, four bedrooms, and three-bathroom wood cabin surrounded by an iron gate. The best that dirty money could buy.

I get out and walk to the house. The van then immediately makes a U-turn and drives off. 'Wonderful' I think as I ring the bell on the intercom at the front gate. I'm involved with too many people that have intercoms, frankly it's annoying.

There's a gravelly, scratchy voice on the other end, "What do you want?"

I don't know what to say, "Yeah, I'm looking for the Commish?" Realizing I shouldn't have said that I make a face. I don't think sometimes before I speak due to the lack of a filter.

"I can tell you what won't get you in to see him kid, is if you refer to him as that again." He tells me what I already know.

At this point I know who I'm talking to. So I stupidly decide to have fun with it. "Help me Commissioner, you're my only help." I giggle to myself at what I think is a funny reference.

I get silence as my response, for a second.

"What could be so important that your friend who dropped you off, left in such a hurry?" He says ignoring that I know it's him.

"It's about the Mayor." I let it out on the table. I'm met with silence once again. "My name is Champ." The gate buzzes. I open and walk to the front door. No one comes to greet me. With a hunch I push and it swings open. "Hello?" I say loud.

"Back here," the same gruff voice as outside says.

I walk towards the back of the house. I come to an office. All the walls and floor are wood paneling. Behind the desk is a wide open window looking out to a mountain side and more trees. The man sitting behind the desk is the only man I still sort of respect, the Commish.

The intercom and a monitor with a view of the front gate is placed to the left of him.

His giant caterpillar mustache sits below his short nose. Underneath his wrinkly brow are his round framed glasses. The wrinkles and his faded bald spot on the back of his head are newer compared to the last time I saw him in person. Especially the lines on the corner of his mouth which look like they came from too much frowning.

In between his first finger and his middle finger on his left hand rests a cigar. I notice a wedding ring on the same hand.

I also notice what he's holding in his left hand along with the cigar, a glass of hutch! I start to make that noise with my mouth. The same one I did in the van, the thirsty sound as I sit down.

"Would you like something to drink kid?"

All I can do is nod my head and utter the word, "drink."

He motions his head to a bar placed in one of the corners of the room. I hustled over there faster than I ever have before. Quickly I make a jack and coke, minus the coke.

"So what's this about kid?"

"You know who I am?" I ask the obvious and silly question. I sit down.

"Yes," he answers it. "I just want to you to know for what's it worth, I'm sorry."

"Then you also know why I'm here." I ignore his apology. Not because I don't accept it but I don't want to acknowledge why he's apologizing.

"The Mayor, he needs to be stopped." It bothers me when the most clichéd, asinine phrases come out of my mouth. I curse myself in my head for sounding like a two-bit movie Marlowe.

"If only you had come to me a few weeks ago." He says as he takes a sip of his drink.

"What does that mean?" To follow suit, I too take a drink but mines a gulp.

He takes a puff from his cigar and exhales some smoke. "It means I've got no more energy left in this kid. I'm spent and drained. That SOB has taken everything I had and everything I was worth."

"I know why your here and you're have every right to give what's coming to him. I would love to help but I'm too old, and frankly I don't care enough anymore. I think it's very noble what you're doing. You give him hell kid; you give him hell." He takes a sip. "I refuse to call that bastard the title he didn't win in an honest race."

I try not to let my emotions get the best of me, especially in situations like this.

Sometimes however like my first meeting with the Mayor it tends to be difficult to keep them bottled up. I find this particular moment one of those difficult times. I'm trying to think of what to say without losing my cool, in the same time coming off sounding powerful and poignant. "Why are you such a pussy?"

While he's in mid drink he stops, raises his bushy eyebrows and looks up at me. "Excuse me?"

I make a serious face. "Let me make this clear, I have a routine of not admitting my true feelings. Some may say it's a bad habit but that's me and I like me. What's the point of getting all emotional if it just makes things worse?"

"With that said, my 'friend' looked up to you for a long time. When he met you that one and only occasion he saw the hero that stood in front of him. It made him want to be the kind of cop you were. The empty shell of a man you have become would crush my 'friend'."

He takes his sip, while he's distracted I roll my eyes and release a nervous exhale. I don't want him to know, my 'friend' was me. "So I was your hero huh?" He says before he even puts his glass down.

"Damn, you know I forgot how good of a detective you were. It's kind of hard to remember that when there's just a big pussy in front of me." I'm trying to light a fire under his ass.

"Wasn't hard to figure out." He puffs some smoke. "That whole 'my friend' spiel is such clichéd bullshit."

"Touché," I say as I think I really wish he was my dad. I keep going, "truth be told I knew you were the voice in the intercom as soon as you spoke." I proudly refer to when I said his name while making that delightful joke. He just shrugs his shoulders but I know he's really impressed.

I get serious, "the plan is to rush his mansion. What I need from you is to hold the cops off for the night. To make sure no one answers any calls to his place."

"I'm tired of this shit kid. I don't have it in me anymore." He takes a breath and then a sip. "Even if I stopped any squad cars from crashing your party, you'll still have to deal with his majesty's inner circle. Do you have any kind of muscle on this?"

"I have muscle; Hermano de Sangre is backing me up." I tell him slightly embarrassed to say that ridiculous name. Also I'm under the assumption that he knows who Blood is.

"Ramirez, that fucking head case?" He says as my assumption turns out to be right. "Be careful with him kid, he's been watching too much Mexican wrestling."

"Tell me about it," I say as I roll my eyes. Then I start to think of something, how far in the know is he? I know he's the Commish, but he doesn't seem particularly assertive when it comes to doing his job. How aware is he on what's been going down?

I swallow the lump that's appeared in my throat. "You knew who I was when I was at the gate. How long have you known of me? Did you know about that night; about what they did to Charlie Polletti's family? What they were going to do?"

He takes another sip and puts out the cigar while staring down at his desk. He doesn't answer right away. He finally speaks but doesn't look at me, still down at his desk. "I heard about you looking into Wulf."

Just the seer mention of Wulf's makes me grit my teeth.

"I also knew when you went to I.A. with what you had on him, after he threatened you."

The truth comes out and not from me. When I told my origin story to Sarah the part I was investigating Wulf was left out. Also was the trip I took to Internal Affairs after Charlie and I were threatened by Wulf.

"I thought you were brave for doing that kid. But also cocky and a little blind. You let your ego and that sense of doing what's right get the best of you. I had that sense, once. Then one day I learned my sense of right is just a candle in a world of darkness. And sometimes that candle can burn you."

"Do you think I'm still that bright eyed, do-gooder whose waves his finger at the bad people," I bark back.

"You want to talk about being put in a situation that shows you that everything you've stood for, everything you fought for isn't worth shit? How about staring at the pile of bodies that you once called a family? Coming to terms at the moment you realize you were the one who put them there?"

"What makes you think I want the Mayor, because it's the right thing to do?"

"That person died in that house years ago. This is about revenge, that may not be as moral as justice but it sure as hell feels better. If you knew, why didn't you say or do anything?" I start to get frustrated because for one thing I hate whining about my problems.

He starts to shake his head. "Kid, I am nothing more than a figurehead. I don't do much. Anything that comes from me got approved by his fatness first."

"Bullshit," I say as my frustration starts to turn into anger over this. I usually don't like to show this much emotion in these situations. The subject matter is making it harder and harder to do that. "I'm sure there are some guys still loyal to you!"

"I told you kid I'm done. I'm the tortoise in a losing race with a rabbit on coke. Even if I had the pull I'm too disgraced for anyone to hear me. The force knowns it."

That curiosity that lays in the bottom of my tummy starts to rise through the bile, the hydrochloric acid and rests at the base of my throat.

"What the hell makes you disgraced? Just because you're the Mayor's bitch now? You gave up caring, I can understand that, but something had to happen for you to feel that way. Or, he's got something on you?"

He starts to roll his eyes around looking around the room. "No, he ain't got nothing on me."

I take a drink. "Seriously, although I don't like to admit it, I was a cop. I know looking around and not at the person talking to you is a clear sign that you're lying. Plus, you made a double negative. So what is it?"

He takes a smoke. "Look kid, we make choices in life that may not always be the best thing for us. You know what I'm talking about."

I'm thinking he's trying to deflect my question by trying to make me remember the stupid crap I did. It isn't going to work.

"So what did you do? Was it a kickback?" He continues to take a drink. I can't really think of anything so I take a stab with a ridiculous comment that's more like a joke. "What did you kill a hooker or something?"

Just then he spits out the drink he had put in his mouth. His face turns white and he has a fearful look in his eyes.

I make my face wrinkle. "Aw come on, fucking hookers?" The last person I thought could pass as a human in this cesspool of a city confirmed my belief that no one is normal.

I am a fool to think he was anything but a stereotypical pervert. That was my last shred of hope that humanity was worth a damn. The voice in my head was right as it usually is. Hell, I really wouldn't call it a shred. What's smaller than a shred, a micro crumb?

"Kid, it's not easy to explain. It's an obsession. Their just so young and innocent, along with being so fragile.

They don't belong on the streets. They belong at home with me, safe and warm. Sometimes I just hold them too tight."

I'm shaking my head in disbelief. Not because of what I learned, but more because I played into it. Then I comprehend with what he just said. "Wait, 'they', you've done this more than once? What's with them being young too? How young are we talking about?"

He starts to nervously pick up his drink. He shakes the glass as he puts it to his lips and swallows slowly. "I'm not going to go into that with you."

That means they were young. I didn't notice before but he has a picture of two women on his desk, one young and one older. I'm guessing his wife and daughter. After he gives me that spiel about not going over it with me he slowly faces the picture frame down.

"Fine, but how many?" I get no answers as he takes a drink. "Three," I take a stab, noting but a drink. I think, "Five," I ask to no response. I jump numbers and take a stab again, "twenty?" his eyes widen but still drinks. I tilt my head back, "fifty"?

He puts his drink down and starts to lose the blood in his face again. "Jesus Christ," is all I can say.

He mouths starts opening like flood gates. "Don't you understand now? That fat fuck he has it all on me. He has pictures, he's even helped me cover it up in exchange for not getting in his way."

I start to think maybe we can work around this. Maybe when we storm the house I can steal whatever evidence he has on the Commish.

Then I start to ask myself do I really want to work with someone like this guy? It's one thing I work with Blood, but the Commish turned out to be a real sick fuck.

Then he says, "You know what, fuck it. I'm gonna stick to that fat fuck one time, before it's too late. Besides, life is short right?" He chuckles quietly to himself. I find to be a tad inappropriate as he picks up the phone. After dialing and waiting a few seconds he starts to talk to someone on the other end.

"Chuck it's me, Fred." There's a pause, "the Commissioner, Fred Chyre. I'm passing on an official command.

Yes, I have done that before. Shut up and listen."

"None of the precincts are to respond to any call coming from the fat man on the hill's house within the next two weeks. Yes, I'm serious. No, no one has a gun to my head. Pass it along Chuck."

"This is a direct order to everyone, even the ones associated with that fuck. I'm counting on you Chuck, that's my wish. Ok, thank you." Then he hung up.

I was shocked although I tried not to show it. I didn't know what to make of that. "I just bought you some time. Chuck is a guy I trust he'll get it done. But, you won't have much time, once it hits fat ass's camp's they'll start beefing up the security. So you have a few days at most." I nod my head.

"Listen kid, like I said you and I weren't that different at first. I was bright eyed, wanted to do the best I could for this city. When I got those medals and junk for helping those people I didn't know why I deserved it."

He swings his chair over to look at his trophy case to his right. "I just thought I was doing my job."

"You should have given them back if you felt like you didn't deserve them." I say half sarcastically. He's still a perv, even though he just helped. What, the guilt got to him finally? A little bit too late I'm thinking.

He ignored my comment. "It started when I was a senior detective. I was working a case where I had to talk to a possible witness who was a prostitute. She was young, looked like my daughters age at the time."

"I remember thinking how could someone let this beautiful angel out of their sight long enough for her to run away from home. I felt bad for her and after my shift was over I went back to her spot which was in a run-down motel. I bought her some food in her shitty room."

He takes a drink. "I just wanted to protect her. So I went over to her. She was stuffing food in her face as if she hadn't eaten in a while which I believed to be true. I held her, then started kissing her, I don't know what came over me. I started on her cheeks and then on her mouth even with the food all over her face."

He takes another drink. "Oh God, I've never told this to anyone. I haven't even thought about it in years. But I have to get this off my chest especially now. I pushed her on the bed and I forced myself...oh God." I do not want to hear this. Luckily he skips the more 'uncomfortable' parts.

"Afterwards, when I got off her, I noticed her face was blue. She was dead. She must have been choking on the food I didn't notice. I know my weight being on top of her didn't help. Jesus forgive me. I didn't do it for a while after that."

Trying not to look at him because I've grown disgusted with this situation I focus my attention on what's outside. The tree swaying in the wind, the warm sunlight coming in through the window into the office, and the glare off the rocks.

"The next one happened a few years later. I had gotten into a fight with my wife and I guess in a way I wanted to get back at her, petty I know." He's still talking like this is an interview with Diane Sawyer, I don't give a shit anymore Joel Rifkin.

I'm more interested in the glare. It's not strong enough to come into the office, but bright enough that I notice it.

"She was so sweet; this wasn't the kind of life for her. When we started having sex I wasn't into it as much as the first girl. The passion was missing, so I started to choke her. She didn't like that."

In the corner in my eye I swear he starts to smirk as he says that part. The glare though it's not coming from the rock, it almost looks like there's someone behind it.

"I swear to you kid, I regret it all. You know kid, I gotta say-," BLAM! Something zips past me and hits the carpet to my right. I look down at the ground and just see a tiny hole with a tiny bit of smoke coming out of it. I move my head to the left looking at the trajectory of where I think the bullet came from.

When I get to the desk I see the Commish sitting there with the glass in his hand and a stunned look on his face. The glass is shattered with shards everywhere and blood pouring out of his mouth. He then slumps over onto his desk. I look outside and there's a small bullet hole in the middle of the window.

Where that glare was coming from is a man, on the mountain side cliff. He gets up and starts to walk away. He moves like Bigfoot in that homemade footage from the seventies. He turns his head around just like Bigfoot to wave at me.

There's what looks like a big smile on his face and then walks off. He's wearing a Hawaiian shirt and has platinum blond hair. I'm amazed he can see me from up there.

"Aw, shit," is the only thing that comes to my mind to say.

The one thing I don't do is panic. I grab a tissue from a box on the desk. I go around the room and wipe down anything I might have touched. I gulp my drink, then wipe down the glass. I go to the bar and wipe down the liquor bottle.

I call Blood to tell him to send the van, he doesn't ask question and I don't say why. Before I leave the room I look at the Commish's body one last time.

With his head slumped down on his desk and blood pouring out of the hole in his throat creating a pool. I think, 'what a waste'. The rest of his drink spilled mixing with the blood and causing a musk smell within the office. This sight formulates the sense of shame inside of me. I get a lump in my throat. It's all very sad.

While walking out the house I wipe down the front door and gate. Then I nervously wait for my ride.

He drops me off in front of my place. I get into my office and I use the burn cell to call the cops anonymously. I inform them I found a body and I describe the Commish's house, then hang up.

I slump down on my couch and stare at my landline. I'm complementing whether I should call and tell Sarah. I finally decide against it. I grab a bottle that was from the floor and drink.

Sometimes when we have stress in our lives the little distractions are the best part of life, even if they are momentary and fleeting. This is my distraction.

The blackouts come soon after. As I slip away I can't help but reflect on that gloomy display. My last thought, 'all that poor spilled hutch.'

5

I slowly creep out of my other distraction, sleep. Quickly my memory of the day before returns. With my eyes closed I run my hand through my hair and replay what happened like a slide show in my brain.

With the Commish there mouth wide open, the ruined hutch, and the blood coming out like a waterfall. The killer, one with nature, waving and smiling. What was that guy the three bong hits said they saw at the bar? What was his name? He said it before he started the ruckus.

I open my eyes and say, "Happy."

Great, another psycho killer who thinks he's a Batman villain on the loose. I look out the window. The sun's not blaring into the office so I'd say it's midafternoon.

I call my new buddy Blood, change my clothes, and get into the van. No blindfold this time, just like when I got dropped off the Commish's house. Blood's trust in me is increasing, lucky me.

At the lair I tell him. He already seems to know. "I know," he says. "Your exploit is all over the news."

"Whoa, whoa, my exploit? I didn't kill him. There was a gunman on the grassy knoll or at least on the mossy cliff. I think his name is Happy. He seems to be an assassin. Most likely hired by the Mayor. He probably knew I was trying to get to him through the Commish."

"Happy," Blood says, "what kind of name is that for a warrior?" Then he makes a scoffing sound and shakes his head as if to say, 'some people.'

"Yeah, well," I roll my eyes, "the good news is the Commish gave us a few days to come up with something. Hopefully we won't have any trouble with the force, as long as they took his last order to heart."

"So let's say we do it in two days. Hey, uh, what day is it today?" I say embarrassed that I don't know.

I look at Blood and he responds with a shrug. He whistles and a goon comes in and tells us "it is Wednesday".

"Perfect," I say. "We'll do it on Friday, say midnight? That's a good time because things can get crazy at that time of night. It's the beginning of the weekend, people coming out of bars, so maybe they'll get distracted."

"Ah, the Witching Hour," says Blood. "Maybe the Gods will smile upon us to make that evening into a full moon."

"Sure whatever, look I'm going. Get prepared to go that night. Get your army together, drench yourself in the blood of the innocent, call Hill just do what you have to do."

"That I will. Then we will form the army of Blood." He then screams, "We will drown the puppet master with his own! Wait," he then says normally, "Blood is confused by something."

"With what," I ask.

"When gringo say Friday on midnight, do you mean Thursday into Friday? Or does gringo mean to say Friday night. Then that would mean Saturday morning." He says with a confused look.

I put my face in my hand. "Jesus Christ, the people I have to work with," I mutter to myself. "Yes, you're right, I mean Saturday morning," I tell him as I lift my head up.

He changes his expression from confusion to a big smile, "excellent, the Witching Hour."

"Wonderful," I say as I turn around and shake my head.

While in the van it dawns on me I'm aware of what my current location is. I wasn't blindfolded when I came here.

Blood's new lair is in another abandoned warehouse in the middle of an industrial district. This discovery deserves a celebratory drink. Although there's never a bad reason for some hutch.

I give an address to the driver that is nearby from here. He drops me off at the corner of Kane St. and Miller Ave. That's right in front of Ceti Alpha V.

Ceti Alpha V is a bar where they tend to play live music. It is a place built by nerds and visited by nerds.

Every Tuesday is the Battle of the Bands. The only rule is every band must reference something from Comic Books, Sci-Fi, or Fantasy. The look, the band name, and the songs have to refer to any movie, book, or TV show nerds love.

For instance, one of the more popular bands are called the Red Shirts. Their four guys dressed up in original series Star Trek outfits. They play songs in the style of early seventies punk to Star Trek lyrics.

I like to go there once and a while to people watch. I enjoy seeing what constitutes as humans nowadays. Most who go are more or less normal looking. There's always that one guy though, who looks like they've never had sex with a woman not to mention talked to one.

Tonight is not Battle of the Bands. Instead tonight it's just a run of the mill rock band. Making an appearance in the middle of their poor excuse of a tour. After the gig is over they'll jam back into the jalopy of a van that was bought for eight hundred bucks. Then it's on to the next garbage heap of a city.

Sometimes up and coming bands will play here. Then sometimes quite the opposite will grace the stage. Tonight is one of the latter.

Normally when sitting at the bar you don't have a good view of the stage. Mainly because there always seems to be a crowd.

Tonight however is different. I can clearly see the band half assing when putting their equipment together. I ask the bartender who's playing because I couldn't dare pay attention to the flyers posted outside. He tells me they go by the name of 'Sexy Snake'.

It doesn't ring a bell. Honestly without even hearing the music by the name alone they sound like a very forgettable band. Turns out they are from the 80's, a hair metal glam band. The bartender hands me the flyer. Apparently they were a big deal in a decade where it was cool to wear acid wash jeans.

On the pink piece of paper is a picture of a woman dressed in lingerie bent over with her ass sticking out. A snake is superimposed to make it look like it's coming out of her butt. It looks as classy as it sounds.

The flyer has a list of what I can only imagine are their 'hits'. Songs like, 'Mouth Full of Love', 'It's Gonna Happen', 'Make the Juices Flow', and their big hit according to the flyer, 'Spread your Legs'. There seems to be a common theme to these songs. I have to admit I'm a little excited now to see this train wreck.

Forty-five minutes pass as they go on late. When the lights come up I almost gasp from what I see on stage.

Imagine Betty Davis from 'Whatever happened to Baby Jane,' but as a 50-year old man. The lead singer's face is caked on with make-up. The eye shadow he's wearing is a deep purple. His face is a powder white which accentuates his bright red lipstick.

However, none of this make-up can cover up the massive amount of wrinkles on his face. Probably brought by drugs, partying, and other great life decisions.

The rest of the band is wearing make-up too but not as much as Tammy Faye.

I love how these 80's bands still think their relevant with their tight leather pants, teased up hair, blouses revealing their chest hair, and make-up. It's ironic to think these guys got a lot of women dressing up as them.

The lead singer introduces himself and the band. "I'm Johnny Dirtbag, whoo!" You said it Gramps. "We've got Tommy Salami on Bass, Scabies on Guitar, oh yeah, and our newest member on drums all the way from Sweden, Heywood Jablüme."

This is just classic I remark to myself. "And. We. Are. Sexy. Snake!!! Yeah, chig-chig-chig-chigacow!!!" Then he begins to move in a slithering motion like a snake as he makes this motion with his mouth, "sssssssss." He counts down and they start singing 'Spread Your Legs'.

"Tonight's the night, you're gonna do what I want you to," sings the potential rapist lead singer.

"Spread your legs," sings the Bassist and the Drummer.

"I'm in your stinky haze." The chorus sung by Johnny Dirtbag.

"Spread your legs," repeated by the other two.

"Your legs make me defecate," provocative and poignant lyrics once again sung by Dirtbag.

This 'song' goes on for another two minutes about a woman's legs and how their attached to such a hot body it makes the man shit himself. All I can do is laugh and try not to drink during the song in fear of spitting it all out.

After their finally done Johnny Dirtbag says to the four people in the crowd, "Who wants to come backstage and get a mouth full of Dirt?"

As to everyone's response, silence. This doesn't stop Dirtbag from thinking he's God's gift to women by gyrating and touching himself during the next song, 'Mouth Full of Love'.

At the tail end of my laughing fit I notice there are actually five people in the audience. The fifth person is hiding by a fire exit under the mezzanine that hangs half way over the audience area. At first I think he's hiding in the shadows because he's embarrassed of just being here which gets me to chuckle.

I take a drink as I continue to look at him because all joking aside his presence makes me raise an eyebrow.

My eyes took a moment to adjust when looking at him because he was engulfed within darkness. His features are starting to come into focus. I now have a pretty good description of him. He's wearing a red and blue Hawaiian shirt, platinum blond hair, and a huge smile on his face.

It's that fucking Happy guy, the one who killed the Commissioner. I almost spring out of my stool. I then keep my composure, take a deep breath, and sit back.

What's he doing here? Is he following me? I've been watching him for a few minutes and he hasn't looked in my direction yet. He just keeps watching the band. Maybe he's a fan? Let's be honest unless you're a fifty-year-old woman who wants to relive her misspent youth, no one's a fan.

I watch him trying to plan out in my head what I'm going to do. The band finishes a song and he applauds, which makes me think there's something wrong with him.

The perpetual smile which causes his teeth to shine out through the shadows and his loud shirt doesn't help. This guy looks deranged, the Mayor sure knows how to pick them.

When the band gets to the bridge of their next song, Happy starts to put his right hand into his semi unbuttoned Hawaiian shirt. This gets me out of my seat again. I don't want to make a move because I can't tell what he's reaching for. This is partially due to the fact that his back is blocking his right arm.

He starts to pull his arm out. This causes me think 'ugh, I guess I have to do this.'

I start moving towards him as quick as I can. That's when I notice what he's pulling out a nickel plated Desert Eagle. My mind starts to wander for a second as I think 'that cannon seems overkill.' Then he fully extends his arm aiming at the stage when I get to him.

I push his extended arm as he pulls the trigger. 'BLAM!' The bullet zips between the singer and the bass player.

Happy looks directly in my eyes and with his big smile he speaks. "Hey Champ!" Then he says, "Did I ever tell you why they call me Happy?" He says it so genuinely, as if he's really glad to see you.

'Oh shit,' I think to myself because I remember that's what he said right before he created pandemonium at the Kamikaze bar.

After his question he swings the hand with the gun back to the position I pushed it from. The butt of the gun smacks me diagonally on the bridge of my nose. I fall back on the floor as he leaves through the fire exit.

I get up as fast I can. I touch my nose and pull back fingers covered in blood as I open the fire exit door. I go into an alley, no other exit but straight. At the end is a tall wire fence. Further down I see Happy. I let off an annoyed grunt because now I have to run.

So I'm hoofing it down this long alley but it's becoming harder to breathe because I think my nose is broken. Happy hears me coming so he turns around and stops right before the end of the alley. I catch up to him and I hunch over from panting.

I raise my hand up keeping one finger up. The universal sign for 'give me a second'. Surprisingly he does. I finally stand up as I remark to myself how can someone as skinny as I be so out of shape?

I finally get a good look at him out in the open up close and in the sun. He's my height, maybe taller. His oversized buttoned Hawaiian shirt covers up his thin yet muscular pale frame.

You can tell he pushes his platinum blond hair back so many times it's perpetually in that position. My eyes quickly scan his medium size side burns which then continues my train of sight to his smile.

That smile, so wide and so bright, radiating sincerity. The kind they make you plaster on your face during picture day. Each tooth is as straight and pretty as the last.

It's a fascinating yet strange one, it's a smile that doesn't come with wide eyes. Not a-I'm-going-to-murder-you-and-wear-your-skin kind of look. It's more like a-I'm-high-on-life sort of look. I think that's creepier than the first one.

I shake my head, snap out of analyzing him, and get back into the game. "I know you were hired by the Mayor to try and kill me but why hire you to kill the Commish and Johnny Dirtbag?"

He looks at me with a smirk. With his head down with what looks like embarrassment he lightly chuckles.

"You got me," he says as he runs his hand through his hair. While lifting his head and stretching his arms out, the eyebrows on his face go up. He smiles and starts to say, "The thing about it is-." In mid-sentence his right hand quickly becomes a fist and thrusts it aimed at me head.

He tried to distract me and it worked. It catches me off guard I try to dodge and deflect it, but I fail miserably. As the ambitious blow connects with my left temple I can't help but think I would have dodged that when I was younger and sober.

I go to throw my right and he pushes it away. He immediately counter punches and it connects to my jaw. Ok, so this guy's obviously faster than me. I get slightly embarrassed from feeling inadequate. As well as being slow and old.

The force of his punch makes me go on one knee. He stands there and says, "What makes you think the Mayor sent me to kill the Commissioner?"

This question adds confusion to my already disorientating brain. Happy takes this opportunity to add salt to the wound by kicking me in the left shoulder causing me to fall on the floor on my back.

He climbs the fence with ease. On the other side he turns half way around to say, "You're right about one thing, the Mayor did hire me to kill you." So I got that going for me.

After he leaves I slowly and sluggishly get up. I feel broken and I just don't mean my nose. Which I have to get set now. What's more stitches must get done for the gash on the top of my nose.

Before I do I can't help but voice a sad observation on something to no one but myself. "He couldn't have been that much younger than me."

At the hospital the doctor has one hand on the tip of my nose and the other on the bridge. Before he pulls and pushes my nose back in place he says, "This is going to hurt."

I respond to him in a monotonous way, "No it's not."

This procedure is oddly relaxing, along with the sowing of the stitches. This is letting me get into the zone and think about what Happy said.

According to him the Mayor did not kill the Commish. Is that a lie? For some reason to me Happy doesn't seem like the kind of guy to lie. As cynical as I can be I do believe he comes off very genuine, albeit extremely unpredictable.

After the hospital I go back to my office. The doctor put a brace and gauze on my nose and gave me some pain medication. The meds get thrown out at the nearest garbage bin. I don't need it for the pain and I certainly don't need it to get my rocks off, that's what the hutch is for. The brace, along with the gauze get chucked out too.

At my place I crash, which includes me prescribing my own kind of medication. I get blotto and eventually reach the blackouts.

6

I wake up from a 24-hour bender. It helped me ignore this gnawing reminder of something I have to do. It's not the fact that the upcoming attack on the fat man's compound could kill me. No, I'm more nervous because it's time to come completely clean to Sarah. Death is easy, it's dealing with the truth that's difficult.

Dying is something I don't tend to think about. Due to the fact that ambivalence towards life has caused this blasé feeling when it comes to the afterlife.

With that said, Friday might be the night where I finally meet St. Peter. That is if you believe in that sort of thing, which I particularly don't. In the case that my body does become a worm feast I have the gnawing feeling I should clear the air with Sarah. No matter how bad that air smells.

I dial her number at the office. As it starts to ring it dawns on me that I shouldn't be spilling my guts over the phone. Not like I did last time, which was tacky. Part of me prefers the phone, less likely to get emotional between the two of us.

As every rings ends and a new one begins I contemplate in person or over the phone? Just as she picks up to say hello, I hang up. I figure if I die or get disfigured at least I'll get to see her face one last time. Maybe as a person compared to as a monster the last time I contacted her.

There's this little voice in my head. It represents the biggest part of my personality. My intuition and BS detector, but also my cynicism. It's the part of me that questions everything.

Right now it's questioning the true reason why I want to talk to Sarah. It feels that by doing this it will trigger lost feelings I had by seeing her. Then that will deter me from leading the seize on the Mayor's place.

Screw that noise in my head, despite it being the most in tuned to my personality out of all my inner voices. I'm not trying to weasel out of what is inevitable. All I'm trying to do is correct whatever wrong I can in my limited amount of power.

Now I know she's at work. I may not know when she gets out but at least I have an idea. I go searching for the alarm clock I own that's buried under a pile of dirty clothes.

Surprisingly it still works.

I learn it's only four in the afternoon. It's difficult to be able to pinpoint when her shift will be over. That would depend on many different variables. I'm just going to take a guess and say I've got at least five hours.

Now I'm forced to do the one thing I don't want to do and that's wait by her precinct. This is my old precinct, the one that got Charlie killed. Who am I kidding, I know who really got him murdered. Typically, I would not get caught dead standing in front of this hellhole. Waiting for Sarah pacing back and forth like some love sick teenager.

I hired a taxi and I'm anxiously sitting in the back seat shaking my leg as we're parked across the street. I've become so uneasy I'm a step away from biting my nails. It's going to cost a bit having the cab parked here for what I think will be a long wait. I don't care about the money; I care more about who may see me.

Three guys start coming out all laughing and talking.

One of them is Wulf. Seeing him standing there sharing a laugh with his buddies invokes a deep rooted hate that lurks to the surface. My face starts to twist with anger. He takes out the toothpick he's always chomping on to presumably tell a joke. It's most likely an offensive one.

What follows is a big collective guffaw from the other two. All the while as they lie in the ground still unavenged.

My hands start to grip the head rest of the passenger seat in front of me. The driver notices my nails are digging into the upholstery.

"Hey, what are you doing?" He says snapping at me.

"I'm making this piece of crap look better." This doesn't make the situation better. If I don't appease this potential problem, he could kick me out and leave me vulnerable in front of my 'nemeses'. That's what we're calling him now.

I calm the driver down by telling him I'm going to stop and give him extra money for the trouble. This calms me down as well. When I turn back to look outside at Wulf again I notice he's gone. I make a mental note that when this is all over I'm definitely going after him and the rest of the Mayor's flunkies.

My thirst for blood and revenge get averted when I see Sarah come out of the precinct.

If my rage for Wulf is like yeast causing a cake to rise, then Sarah became whatever the opposite of yeast is.

I forgot how pretty she was. I haven't seen her since the funeral years ago and that was from far away. Ok in all honesty maybe I stalked her a few times, but that was before I purged most of my nostalgic feelings out.

She stands there fumbling through her over-sized handbag most likely looking for her cellphone. She could recite back to you all of the police codes but can't remember where she put her house keys. With her small 5'6" frame she doesn't look like much of a threat, but her bite is worse than her bark.

Especially when she knows how to knock you down by focusing her force aimed directly at your legs. Then while you're lying on the ground she breaks the delicate part that connects your forearm with the elbow. All the while reciting the scientific terms of the parts of your body she just destroyed.

That ruthlessness counterbalances with her sweet, nurturing, and generous nature. Frankly I haven't seen much of that Sarah lately because I ruined receiving the gift that is her personality.

When I initially pushed her away it was so difficult for me. I missed her humor, we both shared a love for the three stooges. Or her sultry eyes and the way she would look at you when you had a bad day as if to say 'it's ok, I'm here now'. It was all these parts of her that made me fall in love. Her nice ass helps too.

Watching and reminiscing about her is slowly starting to undo all of the brainwashing I gave myself so I wouldn't care anymore.

Even though I stopped thinking about her or caring for her, I could never get rid of the guilt. So that's what this is now. I don't need or want her sympathy. I've already purged those emotions that all those memories brought.

The only thing left is the guilt. I'm not even looking for forgiveness I know I could never receive or accept that. Plus, the guilt will never fully go away. I can never get to say those words to Charlie so maybe I can do it with her.

As painful as it's going to be to do it, this might be my last chance.

I roll down the window and stick my head out to scream out her name. Not the most subtitle way of getting her attention. Especially when the plan here was to keep a low profile.

She comes over to the car and I convince her to have a drink with me. She doesn't want to go to a bar though, prefers going to a diner to get coffee. 'Great,' I think to myself, 'it's about time I get a lingering taste of shit in my mouth'.

Going to the diner across from the precinct is not an option as it is a cop diner.

There's another one nearby that gets suggested as Sarah gets in the car and we go. When she initially got into the taxi I scooted over and went to turn my head.

The intention was to say something sarcastic and cynical. To hide the fact that seeing her unlocked, what's that sensation called that moves around in the pit of your tummy, oh yeah, feelings.

Expect my cunning wit was intercepted with a smell. It was more of a scent. It unlocked memories I hadn't thought of or assumed were long dead.

Turned out it was Sarah's perfume. I completely forgot about that scent. It smelled like, I don't know, a fruit and maybe ginger? Whatever it is it's another forgotten reason why I was into her.

When she looks at me she's startled. I'm facing her with my eyes closed and nose in the air trying to smell this beautiful scent I rediscovered. It becomes too difficult to sense the perfume due to my newly broken nose. Which she now notices.

"What the hell happened to your nose!?" Sarah's original surprised reaction to me sniffing the air converted to immediate concern.

I play it nonchalantly, "you should see the other guy." She looks at my stitched gash and bruised cheeks. "No really, you should see the other, he looks fine." Sarah goes to touch it but hesitates until I reply, "I don't feel it remember?"

She looks at me and just responds with a nod. The taxi propels on.

Sitting across from each other in one of those booths with a mini-jukebox I remark to myself how terrible this coffee is. I told Sarah to order me the same thing she got. I didn't realize that was going to be the special mud flavored crap. I wish I could Irish up this coffee.

Then it dawns on me, why don't I own a flask? I'm supposed to be this clichéd drunk private dic and I don't even own a damn flask. This revelation saddens me. There is going to be a common theme of unhappiness with what I have to tell Sarah.

I decide to just get into it, no more hesitation. "The reason why I asked you out was I wanted to talk to you and be honest about a few things."

"Ok," she says weary about what might come next.

"I know that I wasn't very open when we were together. That I kept my feelings and past close to my chest." She nods as she sips her garbage tasting coffee.

"Well here it goes. I had told you when I was a baby I bit the tip of my tongue off. Well my mother, who already had the typical trepidations of a young new mother had become full blown paranoid. All of her issues that resulted in over-protecting me came to a head when I was in the fourth grade."

"It was a weird time for me. I started getting into that awkward part of growing up. I was not much of a popular kid at that point. Any friends I had I grew apart from. Most of the kids were getting into things like sports while I still played with my collection of Captain Thunder toys."

"Adding to the fact that my mother had informed the school of my condition I became known as the freak. I was an outcast for the outcasts."

"While in gym class there was a rope hanging from the ceiling. So when the gym teacher wasn't looking a few of the kids in my class were playing around with it, trying to climb as high they could."

"Let me guess, you fell." She guesses correctly with her uncanny ability to pinpoint where a story is going. Let us not forget her impatient stance on dramatic storytelling.

"What the hell, Sarah?" I raise my voice as she shrugs her shoulders and sips her mud.

Trying not to let her discourage me I continue with my over dramatic storytelling. "I was lonely and desperate for friends. I decided to impress the kids by climbing all the way to the top of the rope."

"Trying to show off how tough I was I went as far as spitting on my hands before grabbing it. Something I saw being done on TV but not having a clue what it did."

"I learned the advantages of not being able to feel pain that day. Without pain from distracting me I was able to get to the top of the rope. Even got to touch the ceiling. With the kids hooting and hollering I felt on top of the world, sort to speak."

"Climbing down was definitely different than going up. For one, I didn't know how to. That lack of knowledge was my ruin. So in a long form answer, I fell. I don't remember the moment I lost my grip. All I remember is falling far and the sound I made when I hit the ground."

"Everyone crowded around me while I laid flat on the ground. I got up and basically walked away, everyone freaked out. They went crazy, acted like that was the coolest thing they ever saw. In the back of my mind I did worry about maybe seriously hurting myself and not knowing."

"That quickly went away because I was popular for fifteen minutes."

"For an eight-year-old who had no classmates come to his birthday party that's like Heroin, Weed, and the scene in Carrie when she wins Prom Queen combined. Before the Pig's blood."

"I know what's it's like to be unpopular in school." She says as she almost finishes her drink.

"Yeah, but this isn't about you." I shoot a dirty look back at her. She puts up her middle finger. In a playful way, I think.

"Anyway, for the rest of the day I was on a high I never wanted to come down from. I felt accepted, acknowledged, and finally not stressed out about being the loser kid with no friends. I was a very high strung eight-year-old."

"Of course I didn't notice the limp I had produced. Same thing goes for the spot of blood on my pants leg. These got noticed when I got home. I rolled up my jeans and revealed a piece of bone sticking out of my right ankle."

Sarah makes a face of anguish and says "oh god."

"Yeah, I was freaking out, didn't want my mother to find out. I knew this would turn her into more of an obsessed psycho than she already was."

"Now if my mother was the over protective parent than my father was the opposite of that extreme in that he didn't give a shit. For the most part my mother was a single parent."

"As hard as I tried I couldn't hide it from old eagle eyes, she noticed almost as soon as she came home. I think it was my limp that gave it away. The doctor confirmed my worst fears, a severe break in the ankle. So bad in fact if it had gone untreated longer, it was in risk of being cut off."

More horror on Sarah's face. "After that she immediately pulled me from school, quit her job, and started home schooling me. She tried to pursue suing the school despite my father objections. That just became too expensive in the end."

"I found out later that she had planned on the home schooling even before my accident. She was converting part of the house into a classroom."

"I wasn't allowed to play any sports anymore after that. Going outside for recreational reasons became scarce."

"My social life or there lack of became pretty non-existent. It was a tough time. My comics, movies, and books helped me through it. As well as the growing obsession with Captain

Thunder, who was practically my only friend."

"I'm sorry you were so lonely growing up. Did you get home schooled all the way till the twelfth grade? That must have sucked."

I know that if I was on the receiving end of this sappy origin story I'd be making some tacky joke, not Sarah though. At least I know she cares despite my jerky personality.

"It did and after graduating the high school which was my home I wanted to leave for college. Even though I was practically an adult my mother wasn't having that. She had stopped me from having a normal life once again by secretly applying me to a local community college."

"Looking back at it now I understand why she did what she did. Mom sacrificed a lot to provide me with a good education. She did a good job too."

"Sometimes the jokes you hear about being homeschooled aren't just misconceptions. Not with mom though, she tried to make it fun and informative. I know I got a better education from her than I would have in a brick and mortar school."

"Despite her hard work, there's still a negative connotation with being taught by your mommy. Plus, it's not something colleges want to see on applications."

"I'm still bitter with her turning me into the boy in the bubble. She might have done a great job with my intellect, but for all of her books and teachings it couldn't help me with human contact. I wasn't doing that at college."

"Becoming free from what I thought was my mother's reign of imprisonment was becoming more important than making friends. One day I came to the realization that the key to my locks was either joining the military or becoming a cop."

"I quit school. When my mother found out she was not happy. When I told her I was joining the academy, there are no words powerful enough to describe how upset she was. I remember she slapped me. After immediately feeling terrible about it she ran off and didn't speak to me for months."

I take a sip of my coffee since my throat is getting dry from talking so much. I make a face as I put the cup down. It didn't help with the dryness it just left a strong bitter taste in my mouth.

"So you made it into the academy, must have been a culture shock for you. Even though you had some experience being around a large group of people. That's still a lot more testosterone than you were used to." The more I'm around her the more I remember why I liked being around her. I hate getting sappy.

"Exactly, I went from an awkward kid and was turning into an awkward man. I didn't know how to talk to people or how to make friends. Joining what was basically a huge group of frat guys with guns was the worse place to learn how to do that."

"I always took solace in books and studying since it was the only thing I was good at. The analytical part came easy since I had a sharp memory and a natural ability of solving problems. It was the physical part of it that was tough."

"Mom being as paranoid as she was made me go through this regiment before going to bed. Basically I checked my body for cuts, bruises, and broken bones. Then in the morning I had to stretch to prevent pulling or damaging something."

"That's terrible." She says as the waitress who I've named Alice in my head comes over to refill our cups. I wasn't fast enough to put my hand over my cup to indicate I didn't want a refill. I am now forced to drink more of this swine. "Do you still do that every day," She asks.

"I try, but sometimes things get in the way." It gets a bit awkward after that. As she takes a sip from her cup I am reminded of drinking some hutch. I break this silence, "my mom was fucking crazy for coming up with that. Despite the fact the regiment seems a bit much, she had a point in making me start it."

"Case in point it helped me keep safe from injury while at the academy. I took my time as much as I could when it came to the physical stuff but it still made me nervous."

I take another sip of this gross crud. I realize being with her is making me soft. A few months ago I never would have stood for drinking this crap. I shake off this idea and continue with the sob story.

"When the day came where I graduated from the academy I was top of my class but that's not what was on my mind."

"Being at the academy may have made me feel free for the first time but still I had no friends. Like a Gorilla being released into the wild I was still so apprehensive about the real world. I tasted the forbidden fruit of freedom but I was still that shy book nerd. I brought that personality to my first precinct."

"The good old 108th," Sarah says halfheartedly to herself with a smirk on her face. The expression seems to represent not found memories but more similar to thinking back to a friend who caused more trouble than they were worth.

I respond with nothing self-significant than a grunt. "Yeah, the 108th precinct became my home away from home. Unfortunately, it being the real world this did not clash well with my nerdy nature. Neither did being around even more testosterone fueled power hungry frat boys with guns."

After taking another sip Sarah half laughs, "Try being one of the few women in that zoo."

I shake my head, "I know but this isn't about the plight of the woman in the work force." She gives me a sarcastic smile.

I continue with my long rant in which I'm just avoiding the inevitable. "I hated the other beat cops I was being partnered up with. Most of them reminded me of the bullies I grew up with."

"It only made me strive harder to become a better cop. Even though that made me more of a target of not being very well liked. Through the work I became a junior detective where I was parented with Charlie."

I abruptly stopped talking. Mentioning his name at this point gives me a lump in my throat.

"Are you OK?" Asks Sarah as she takes her hands off her coffee cup and slowly moves them over to my hands which start to tremble slightly. I'm not even paying attention.

The daze that has consumed me has diverted my staring eyes away from our table. It takes me a second to snap out of it and realize she's touching me. Her warm smooth hands come to a complete shock to me as I haven't touched anything that wasn't a cold glass bottle in forever.

Plus, for it to be her touch, it's an experience I had long forgotten. This causes me to instinctively draw my hand back quickly as if it had just been touching an open flame. Not because I didn't like it, more because I don't deserve it.

Sarah doesn't know this, so she casts a bit of an offensive expression on her face. It doesn't last long as she quickly ignores it and tries to make me feel better with her words instead. "I know talking about him upsets you and that you think you blame yourself but you don't have to." She says sympathetically.

I swallow my lump. "That's the thing, it is my fault." I say which seems like I'm going to tell her everything but I quickly dance around it. "Charlie was the nicest cop I ever met. He was a great guy and partner. He knew that I focused on my career too much and this made me an unhappy person.

At this point I was pretty much done trying to make friends. He took pity on me but he never thought of it that way. I was so introverted and socially inept. Add to the fact that I was hiding the truth about my medical condition which made me feel even more isolated."

"He opened up his home, his life to me. I never thought I could be accepted or allow myself to feel that way. I eventually became part of the family even if I was reluctant in becoming accepted." I stop to take a drink of coffee and not because I have dry mouth or I'm thirsty. It's because I'm punishing myself for sounding like such a wuss.

I just hope I don't compare not having friends to my **Congenital Analgesia**. "I had sometimes felt that my **Congenital Analgesia** not only kept me numb from pain but from human contact as well." Jesus Christ just shoot me now; I've become everything I hate.

I keep treading on. "Charlie introduced me to Tina and the kids pretty early on. It was a way to help open me up, it eventually worked.

Like I said and as you already know I became part of the family. If Charlie became my brother, then Tina was like my sister. I don't usually like kids because I can't connect with them, but the twins-." I will not say their names I draw the line with them.

"They were fucking cool kids. When they started calling me Uncle-." I feel that lump rising back into my throat. I will not let it do me in, this is not a Lifetime movie. I just keep going maybe she'll just think it's too much of an emotional subject to talk about. She would be wrong about that though, really.

She goes to touch my hand again, but before she can I move away. "Why do you keep doing that?" She asks in an annoyed tone.

I look down and say reluctantly, "I don't deserve it."

"What, my hand?"

"Your affectation."

She raises her voice slightly, "don't be ridiculous. Is this because of how the way things ended between us? I'm getting over that especially after everything you told me."

I decide I'm tired of this holding back, I need to answer for I've done. Screw the consequences, why am I so worried about how she's going to react? I deserve whatever comes at me. It's better than her feeling bad for me which just makes me feel guiltier.

I pick my head up and let the cards fall where they may. "I don't deserve your affection or your sympathy. It's because I am the reason why Charlie and the family you and I came to love are dead."

She pulls her hand back that was still left on the table. "What the hell are you talking about?"

"That's the other secret I never told you aside from my medical problem. I mentioned Wulf was involved. He ran a protection ring on a bunch of local businesses. He had a crew of other cops working under him."

"A rookie never learns that just about everyone is shady as shit and no one does anything about it. That includes the most standup guy I had ever met. When it came to the corruption in the precinct Charlie wouldn't touch it with a ten-foot pole. He had too much to lose. I didn't understand that then."

"What does this have to do with Charlie's family?" She asks strongly with suspicion; she has an idea where this going.

"I started a file on him, Wulf. It started with writing down whenever he boasted about buying something new. Like how every nine months it would be a new car. Then when I got some hard evidence that he was spending more than he was earning I started researching deeper."

"What kind of evidence?" She asks once again weary for the answer.

I'm tired of dancing around my mistakes I want to be as straightforward as I am when I am insulting people. "I broke into the records department and got a hold of his folder." I say slightly ashamed but looking into her eyes.

"Jesus," she says as she puts her face in her hand.

"Hey, it's not that much more than what you might have done." I immediately regret saying.

She takes her hand away. "Anything I did that was for you." Raising her voice.

"Ok, your right." I quickly try to appease the situation. "This isn't the point. I know I was brash, stubborn, and holier than thou. I felt like Wulf represented the ignorant bullies. I wanted to punish him. How dare he bring his corruption into our precinct. I began to cherish that place because that's where I met Charlie and you."

My week attempt to butter her up so she doesn't hate me after I'm done.

"Anyhow I told Charlie, who did not react well to it. He threw me up against the wall. He didn't want to have anything to do with this because of fear for his family. Even after I tried to assure him that I wouldn't involve him he called me an idiot."

"He said that even if I leave his name out of it he will still get blamed because we were partners. I didn't listen, I was full of myself and so stubborn."

Sarah shakes her head slightly, "What happened?"

I start to turn my head not being able to look at her. "Like I said, I was stubborn. I was also determined so I found Wulf collecting money from local places and maybe, I took some pictures."

She sits back in response, looks down and shakes her head as she says, "Oh no."

"Eventually Wulf found out." Sarah looks up at me hanging on my next word. "He didn't do anything," I say trying to reassure her. "He wasn't happy though and threatened that 'I wouldn't want anything bad to happen if I continued this'."

"I knew Charlie never said anything. All the threats just made me more pissed off. Instead of teaching me a lesson it only made me want to nail his ass to the wall even more. So despite all of my better judgment, I went with my emotions and told I.A."

Sarah gives me a very serious look, a cold look painted on her face. She asks me, "How did you know the bodies were dragged? You mentioned that the last time you spoke about this. And you never told me how you knew there were multiple people there. How did you know?" She has an idea of the answer.

I take a deep breath, everything I am and represent now are all because of the words I'm about to say. "Wulf did it with nine others, all cops. They murdered the kids, assaulted and murdered Tina in front of Charlie. Dragged all the bodies to the first floor. Then beat him to death."

The hardest thing I've ever had to say. I never spoke those words out loud before. I'm staring into space as I talk, gritting my teeth between every word. My face is twitching.

Sarah is breathing heavy through her nose. She hesitates asking her next question with fear in her eyes. "How do you know that?" A tear is forming on the bottom of her eye.

"I woke up abruptly that night with somebody in a ski mask standing at the foot of my bed. Just to knock me out. My eyes opened in a haze. It took a second to comprehend where I was. Looking around with half opened eyes I recognized that I was in Charlie's living room."

"Moving my head around scanning where I was ended with the pile of bodies in the middle of the floor. There was Charlie bloodied, beaten to the brink of death, gasping his last breath."

"Suddenly the hair on the back of my head was grabbed and I was pulled up by it. There was a voice behind me telling me this was my fault. I had let this happen. Then I was told to stop my investigation or more people I loved would die."

"To make sure I understood my head was pushed towards the mess I created. One of the others took a picture which I still own."

This is so difficult for me to say but you wouldn't know it by the expression on my face, it's blank. Until I say, "I know all this Sarah because I was there, because I went to I.A." A single tear rolls down my otherwise blank face. "I thought it wouldn't get out but it didn't matter, they have ears everywhere."

Sarah's face gets wrinkly then tears start to run down her face. She puts her head down because she doesn't want me to see her cry. I know it's not because it may show a sign of weakness but merely because I don't deserve to see her sad.

She looks back up, "how could you, being selfish as usual! This is your fault, I loved them too," she screams those last two parts.

It causes me to look away due to shame. If her being loud caused anyone else in the diner to take notice, I couldn't tell for I didn't care.

There was a silence for a long moment. She sobbed as I looked away. Eventually she started to speak, slowly. "I remember around that time you were becoming distant towards me. Like you were distracted. We would be talking and your focus would be reverted to something happing around us, a fight between a couple."

"It wasn't because you cared either. It was your way of avoiding from having to tell me what you were doing. It all makes sense now. I was so mad at you for so long. You could have come to me. But no, you had to do it on your own."

"You have every right to pissed at me. I don't expect your forgiveness. I just wanted to tell you the truth."

This next part I tell her is not for her to forgive me but maybe it will calm her down. The truth is I want her validation for what I'm going to do tomorrow night.

"That cop I had you look into, Simbudyal, he was one of the ten that was there that night. He was also the one who took the picture. He gave out a lot of information on our esteemed Mayor, not willingly of course. That man is behind all of this. Tomorrow will be the end of it. It will be the end of him."

"What's happing tomorrow? Are you going," wiping her eyes she leans in and whispers, "are you going to kill him?"

I sit back and act like that's a ridiculous statement. "Not me, but rather the party I keep."

"Who," she asks as if to say I sound ridiculous.

I exhale slightly embarrassed by saying, "Hermano de Sangre."

She raises her voice a bit. "What," it goes down a little, "I thought that guy was an urban legend."

I make a short laugh. "No I assure you he is quite real. He was also a cop, Victor Ramirez."

"He sounds familiar. So what now?"

"We part ways. I either never see you again in which I'm sorry for everything." Last time I ever say that. "I'll speak to you soon." I reach my hand out and gently place it on top of hers which takes all of my effort.

"Forgiveness was never something I was looking for. Just if tomorrow is my last day, the truth is what was needed to be set free. They threatened you, the way things ended between us is because you were in danger. I just wanted you to know that."

I take my hand off of hers, get up from the booth, and leave the diner. I now need to purge some feelings again with a lot of hutch.

I head for the 82 bus that will drop me off near my building. I'm not exactly near that bus so I have to take another bus first. I let my brain rest while I'm on the first bus.

Sitting on the bus I am exhausted. Emotional after what I went through, but it quickly converts into physical exhaustion. Without realizing how heavy my eye lids became I start to doze off...

7

Something inside me screams to wake up which is a good thing too because I almost miss my stop to make the transfer. Must have had been snoozing for no more than fifteen minutes.

By the time I've made the transfer to the 82 all I want to do is rest in the back of the bus until I get home. Despite my power nap I'm still tired. Probably a result of my all hutch diet. The idea of resting my head on the window sitting in the back has become a piece of comfort to me.

One could imagine my disappointment when I see a bum festered itself in the back of an entirely empty bus. Bad enough it's situated in the back, but its sitting in the middle of the back row of seats blocking the two corner seats. It is in the way of my relaxing.

Sure I could just go around it, however I'm sure it smells. I could also sit somewhere else next to a window. The rest of them are two seaters and I don't want the potential to being smushed next to anyone.

I settle for a group of seats facing the backdoor of the bus. They also diagonally face that last row of seats where that bum who, big surprise, does smell is in the corner of my eye. At first I just shoot a look of contempt at it. I keep referring to this person as 'it' because the identify of gender is nowhere to be seen.

Their wearing a long oversized coat that almost touches the ground. Under the coat is a hoodie that covers their head. The pull strings are pulled at its tightest so all I see is a nose and that's barely.

My attention goes from the homeless thing to important matters like drinking. Still rearing from the heart to heart crap I had invites for one desperately.

My mind starts to wander between topics. I think of Sarah and the feelings her memory give me. Oh how much I want to drown them. I then get diverted and start thinking about tomorrow.

Tonight might have been the last night I see Sarah. I think about the fates of the Commissioner, Herodes and his sweet, poor little girl. Blood and the Mayor pop into my head with their quest for power. I'm reminded of Powers or Simbudyal, how I ruined his life and I don't feel bad about it.

My thoughts then wander to Happy, the homicidal manic with a positive disposition. How I know seeing him tomorrow is inevitable. I have no clue how I am going to deal with that. Then my thought deviates about flasks, how I should have one, and where do I get one?

Then while reflecting within myself I get distracted by what's happening in the corner of my eye.

The bum starts to move. There's a ruffling in the oversized buttoned down coat. I begin to turn my head while all the buttons start to tear apart seemingly at once. Both sides of the coat swing open almost in slow motion to reveal, Happy.

In his left hand is a giant hunting knife. With his hood down smiling that obnoxiously genuine grin, the kind that shows all of his teeth he's sweating. "Hiya Champ," he says positively. His right hand grabs the tip of the hunting knife, brings it up over his head, and throws it in my direction.

Luckily at this point my head is fully turned around facing him. I see the knife flipping in the air towards my face. I manage to dodge it in time.

As it zips by I turn around to see where it landed. It perfectly struck the signal strip that was behind me causing a loud 'ding'. Which he then immediately says as I turn back to face him, "how's the nose?"

I jump up from my seat and go towards him. I have to try to think like him which means don't think at all, act on instinct. I improvise by grabbing the poles on either side of me and using them to push myself towards him. My right foot flying at his face as he's still sitting.

Moving unbelievably quick he rolls to his right while my foot misses him and hits his empty seat instead.

Left in a position with my leg stretched out I'm cursing myself because now he's going to try to break my leg. In true wildcard style, he doesn't. What he does do instead is he bends down a bit and throws a right jab directly at the most recently vulnerable area, my junk.

It doesn't produce the result he was looking for, although I will probably piss blood later. The missed opportunity for pain gives me the time to get out of my silly position.

Standing there he's dumbfounded as to why that didn't work. What is created is a small moment of awkwardness as we stand across from each other just staring.

The confusion on his face washes away. "Oh right, I stupidly forgot," he says with a half smirk on his face while shrugging.

Now I have the look of confusion. He knew about my condition just forgot for the moment in the heat of battle? We're still standing there in uncomfortable silence. He's in a wrestling position as if he's waiting for me to make the first move.

So I decide to but not the kind he probably expects. "Why didn't you try to kill me before in the alley?"

"I like the theatrics," he says with a smile and raised eyebrows.

I think between this schmuck and the other schmuck in face paint I'm surrounded by Drama dropouts. It then dawns on me I don't see his cannon of a gun with him. I wonder if he even brought it.

At that moment the driver jerks the bus abruptly to the right. My attention stupidly gets distracted. The only other person on this bus is changing lanes and getting closer to the next stop due to Happy's knife. Not only to mention he has not reacted to our noisy fight once.

My being distracted gives Happy the opportunity to kick me dead in the stomach. This doesn't hurt but rather takes the wind out of me. As I hunch down from the force he heads for the knife that is still stuck on the signal strip. I tackle him before he can.

I knock him into some seats. I get off and am about to make a move when the bus driver hits the brakes. This causes me to lose my balance. I almost fall until I grab on to something.

Happy quickly gets up and jimmies his knife out of the tape. We both stand up and are facing each other again. He starts to look over my shoulder since my back is facing the front of the bus.

"I told him not to pick anyone up." Foolishly I look behind me due to my curiosity. A women carrying a stroller with two kids, who look young, just got on the bus. I turn back to Happy when he says with a short chuckle, "I even paid him."

This seems to calm him down a bit as he puts the knife down on a seat behind him. I get confused, don't tell me this psycho doesn't want to use a very dangerous weapon because kids are on board? What kind of crazy killer is this?

At this point I know I have to get out of here. The bus hasn't left the stop yet so this might be my only chance. While his body is slightly turned away from me I manage to grab the hood from his hoodie.

I violently pull it over his head. While holding it down with my left I start throwing my right aimed at his head, face, whatever.

The bus starts pulling away from the stop. I know this is it. I let go of his hood, give him a heavy push, and start heading for the front of the bus. I can't go through the back door because the bus is in motion. So now the only way to get out is to do the two things I don't like doing, running and yelling.

"Stop the bus, stop the bus," I am screaming bloody murder. Running down the aisle passing the mother and her kids, the bus driver is shocked to hear my cry. He stops the bus which causes me to almost fall again.

I haven't looked back, I don't know what Happy is doing and frankly I don't care I just want to get out. When I pass the driver I say to him sarcastically, "you should get a raise."

He gets the door open but with everything going on trying to frantically get away, I trip. I fly out of the bus and crash onto the sidewalk hard making a loud popping sound.

I quickly get up and start running. I stop when I think to myself, 'why am I running?' I know he didn't get off. His setup was ruined with that lady and her kids getting on. A killer with a heart of gold who won't kill women or children.

This now puts me in the predicament of having to walk home. Despite that pop sound I heard everything seems to be working fine. I won't know for sure till I do my nightly routine.

When I get back at my place as soon as I sat down I fall asleep. Outside the loud snapping sound of a car backfiring wakes me up and puts me in a sense of panic and dread. I take the opportunity of being awake to wash up and check myself for bumps and bruises. My left knee feels weird have to examine it later.

I cautiously go out to get some hutch. Then I do my somewhat daily routine of drinking until I get to the blackouts. Same shit different day, I just hope this won't be the last time. Well at least I won't be thirsty during the big battle. I bought a flask, turns out they sell them cheap at the liquor store.

8

I wake up the next, I don't know, midafternoon? From what I can tell based on how the sun isn't blaring into the office. My eyes open reluctantly as it dawns on me today might be my last day on earth.

How over dramatic of me to even suggest that. I don't really believe it will be my last. Although it might be if I don't do something about Happy. I don't know anything tangible about him, other that he's a fucking loon. I doubt that's his real name, people and their stupid nicknames.

I don't really have enough to go on. That insane person must have been riding that bus line back and forth waiting for me. He knew about my condition most likely from the Mayor.

I'm sure he had an idea where I was. Would not be surprise if he's followed me from time to time. I should have noticed but I have been distracted. Who am I kidding I've been to drunk and lazy to care.

When checking myself I see that the left knee is swollen. That's the one I banged jumping out of the bus. I massage it which is all I can do at the moment. I don't even have ice. I will have to remember to buy a wrap for it and some ice.

I check my nose which is still broken, bruised, and stitched. I didn't hit it at all when I made my dramatic escape. I decide, perhaps unwisely, to not bandage my nose. I feel it will just get in the way.

While getting dressed I wonder what to do on my potentially last day on earth. I look for my blade; I find it in between the cushions of my couch must been there for a while. I also make sure I have my tape recorder on me.

I've decided to do something I don't normally do, bar hopping like a hipster. I got my blade, the evidence, my flask filled, money in the shoes, and I'm out the door.

As I walk down the stairs and into the streets I feel ambivalent about tonight. I'm not scared nor do I want to run. Do I want to die? I honestly don't know. I definitely don't want to die by those fat and sweaty hands.

The first spot is Camp Crystal Lake, or CCL, as called by no one. It's designed to look like the set of a movie that shares its name with the unluckiest day of the year. For me that's called every day.

I figured I just recently visited a Sci-fi themed bar, why not a horror one. I do enjoy the countless number of themed bars this city seems to possess.

The inside looks like the campgrounds. In the middle of the open room is a fake campfire with benches surrounding it so you can sit and drink. There's a sitting area that's made up like the front of the cabin. Area's also have a certain hockey mask wearing machete welding maniac poking his head up and around.

For example, the bushes near the campfire. He also shows up in a mock window that's in the bar's bathroom. A popular one is a display where he's holding a sleeping bag with a squirming body inside. Their all mannequins strategically placed.

I enjoyed watching horror movies when I was growing up. Despite all the dismay of my mother, I snuck in all the viewing that I could. As I told Sarah, horror movies, books, and Captain Thunder were my only outlets.

I forgot to mention the two rooms in the back facing opposite of each other. Their small and private, the left one is the Romero room and the right the Argento room. Both have various pictures and memorabilia from their respective movies. I've always been more receptive to the movies from the left room myself.

With not much going on at CCL, this does not stop me from pounding them back. I've taken my great idea of having an all-night party of one and in typical Champ fashion got lazy and too drunk.

My first clue when I learned I was too wasted to continue bar hopping? That would have to be when I was pissing in the fake bushes thinking I was really in a forest.

The man in the mask peeking through gave me so much of a startle that I punched him in the plastic head. I snapped out of my drunk stupor when the bartender started yelling at me. I took my leave hopping out of there in mid pee.

I decide to wobbly walk to my place hoping to get some rest before I am called into battle. Never even made it inside. Was a lot more wasted than I thought I guess.

9

A blare from a car horn forcibly wakes me up. Turns out the car is a van, it's also feet from my head that was in a peaceful sleep seconds ago. The reason why I ended up so close to this vehicle is because I passed out in my alley, on a mountain of garbage.

I am now forced to slide out of my comfy garbage bed, which I do begrudgingly. This becomes very difficult to do. Due to the fact I am still very drunk.

Eventually heading inside the van I look at the clock and notice it is only eleven. The revolution is starting early.

Sitting in the front passenger side we drive through some of the city. I can't help but reminisce on some of the things that have transpired of late. We pass the alley behind the Double Down Saloon, where I found the body that started this all.

Zipping by the 108th I become aware that it did not start with finding that body.

Passing the filth of the city and coming to the 'nicer' parts of town we go down a street that would eventually lead to Power's house. More suitably his former home as I heard he was kicked out when his wife found out about his extracurricular activities. Most likely forward to her by his former cop buddies.

Making the exit on the highway crawling towards the gates of Kalani I can see the neighborhood where Charlie's family lived. Trying to look away with a heavy heart I can see the mountain tops that surround the city.

They remind me of the Commissioner and then of Happy. When I do a chill goes down my spine.

Before making that final ascent to the Mayor's castle top we drive past the Herodes manor.

I can tell myself I don't care. That I put up a cement wall surrounding my heart, but every wall has cracks. Astra never asked for this nor does she deserve it. If any emotion other than anger and hate should be dedicated to anyone it has to be that little girl. Except for her dog, shithead bit me.

I take a swig out of the flask and we finally make our way up to see the king of sleaze.

As the van slowly makes its way because of the steep road I can't help up look back at the skyline of our fair city. I remark to myself how much I hate it. How I thought moving here from my parents back in north bumblefuck Middle America was the right choice.

You come here with starts and dreams in your eyes. Then the first drug addict gangbanger comes and scoops those eyes out with a rusty spoon.

Ok, that may not be autobiographical, it's just an analogy. The point is this city will steal whatever you held sacred and rapes it.

I made my choices and I don't put blame on anyone else but for myself. With that said, this place has a bad influence on you. Look at the Mayor, I'm sure he wasn't always a fat greedy slime bag. Then again, we will never know.

The van stops yards before we get to the Mayor's gate. We make a sharp left into the woods. We drive through some trees and stop in a clearing where there are other cars and vans parked with their high beams on. We get out and I see Blood standing in front of an open trunk of a car.

I stumble over to him, "What's the plan?"

He turns around revealing inside the trunk, an arsenal of weapons. In his hands is an RPG, he then answers my question by saying, "We are going to blow the shit out of his house."

I stand there shocked, "Jesus Christ. Talk about overkill."

"No, you look up there." He says pointing at the massive amount of mortar, brick, concrete, marble, and whatever other expensive building materials that monstrosity is made out of. "He is the one that has built his mansion in the sky with the blood of the working man."

"Give me a break Che Guevara." I say as I shake my head. I do look up to see what he's saying as I can see the house but in a different angle, the back of it. I only saw the front and I know how excessive the inside is, but am surprised when I see the back. "Is that a grotto?"

Blood turns from me to address his followers; he breaks my attention as he speaks.

"My fellow warriors, tonight under the full moon we climb up that hill of oppression and claim what is ours. What belongs to every citizen of this city? Tonight we become liberators, tonight we cut the strings that bind us, and tonight we free ourselves from the reign of the titiritero, the puppet master!"

In typical Blood fashion he yells that last part. I'm left shaking my head in this sea of stupidity. All of his soldiers that drank the Kool-Aid cheer him on. I can't help but reflect on how most of them are young and all of them are males.

I guess it's true what D-nice said, all the woman are just treated as concubines. Their probably back at home base waiting for their young, male fighters to come back so they can reward them with sex.

I'll give it to Blood, to recruit young. That's the only way you would be able to manipulate someone to go through this stupid idea. Except for maybe revenge, that's a pretty good reason too.

After his speech Blood turns to me again and walks closer. "How are we with the reinforcements for the pigs?"

"As far as I know the Commish in one of his last acts set it up that we won't be disturbed." I say forgetting about that guy. I've been so out of it the past few days, did his death even get released yet?

Then it dawns on me I forgot to tell Sarah about that little nugget of info. "I cannot guarantee that anyone on the Mayor's death squad won't be called in as soon as we start storming the walls."

"Understood," he answers looking at the mansion.

"By the way," I start to ask, "where's Hill, is he going to join us on this beautiful night?"

He smirks at me, "dear Hill cannot risk to show his allegiance with the right just yet. He does however bless us with the finest gifts known to blow the holes into the carcasses of whales."

He says as he points to all the weapons that are being carried and handed out. Other than the aforementioned RPG's, there are assault rifles, machine guns, shotguns, and even grenades.

"There is one more thing that needs to be discussed before we split the night with war." The over dramatic baby says to me, which leaves me puzzled. "This man, the harbinger of death that you call, Feliz."

Now I really become confused, Feliz? My limited Spanish helps me figure out what he's talking about. "You mean Happy?"

"Si, Happy, this must be dealt with by you."

"Me, why the hell me?" I ask him acting like I had not already planned on dealing with Happy.

"Because that is what the Gods call upon you to do. You two warriors are intertwined, equally strong, equally dangerous."

"Fine, stop trying to butter me up. How did you know about Happy anyhow?"

"I see all and I know all," he says as he walks away from me. Why do I bother?

Blood struts to the middle of the circle created by the parked vehicles with his body pointed at his target, the house. Drenched in bright light he screams, "to me my warriors of the night."

Everyone follows death machines in hand to the center standing near Blood. All but me as I stand there unmoved with apathy on my face waiting to hear what nonsense this schmuck is going to say next.

"It is time; you all will move on to the next level. Which one depends on you. You can go from warrior to a slave of death or you can go from warrior and become my brother! Now is the time we unleash hell!" Thanks Gladiator, and of course he yelled that last part.

No surprise this amp's everyone up. During the screaming and celebrating one of them breaks away from the group. He lifts up what I can only imagine is a heavy RPG. He then fires a rocket that slams into the concrete wall surrounding the Mayor's fortress.

As the wall explodes pieces of rocks from big to small fly up into the air. We're lucky enough to be far away that none of the debris comes close.

The noise however is so loud my hearing gets muffled and causes the ground to shake. The act even gets me to flinch and put my hands on my ears, little good that did.

With perfect timing immediately following the explosion thunder and lightning start to form from the sky. The rain starts to fall as Blood screams, "a sign from the Gods our time of war, death, and winning has come to us. Let us not disappoint them!"

This causes the group to get even crazier as they all start to charge the hill and seep through the hole that was just created. Like an army of ants trying to take down an elephant. There are many and fast but the enemy is large and powerful.

The painted up homicidal clown that is Hermano de Sangre leads his army in the back. He is slowly making his way to the opening in the wall. All the while smiling as his face paint starts to drip off due to the rain. He acts like a proud papa just seeing his big baby boy who's so full of potential for the first time.

I hang back behind them, letting all the brainwashed go in first. Drinking from my flask I eventually make my way up the hill, then through the concrete opening.

Shortly after a second explosion is heard. This one is closer so the noise causes ringing in my ears. It also knocks me back as it took me by surprise. The ground shakes harder this time and the whole thing has caused me to be disorientated.

I start to stumble behind the house trying to take refuge and rest from the explosion fucking with my head. The back of the mansion is more extravagant than the front or the inside. A giant pool the size of a lake. I mentioned the grotto with a waterfall but not the slide.

I sit down on the side of the pool wondering why the waterfall is still on because of the rain.

My head in my hand with the other one pushing my ears in trying to get the ringing to stop. I may not be able to feel pain but that doesn't mean I am pervious to tinnitus.

I start to think how any of the others could stand such a head assault and still be gung ho for blood. Then I'm remind that they have a lethal combination of adrenaline and Blood's manipulation in their blood.

I start to feel better as I prepare myself for this slaughter. I have to find Happy and finish this. I take a drink then I slap my thighs which are getting soaked by the rain, "Ok, let's do this."

As I'm about to get up I hear this splashing sound in the pool. Then these two arms come from seemingly nowhere wrapping themselves around me. I hear a voice originating from the same place as the arms. It says those two words that produces a horror that shoots down my spine, "Hiya Champ!"

Happy's arms start to squeeze around me. His grip is like a vice. Why is it everywhere I turn there he is and how long did he stay underwater? Happy uses his grasp to his advantage by trying to drag me into the water. I know if I go under, I'm done.

I grab the edges of the pool and hang on tight. The good thing about this situation is I don't have pain to distract me from trying to win this tug of war. The bad thing however is there is a lot of water involved which is causing me to lose my grip.

I don't think his arms are long enough to keep his hold on me especially since I keep trying to get out. His grip starts to get looser just as the hold my right fingers had start to go. I get the idea to elbow him in the face. This becomes easier said than done.

We're both struggling and moving around violently. Chlorine water is splashing everywhere and the rain isn't helping. This makes it hard to see. All of this becomes a factor in why I'm not connecting with any part of him.

My arm starts to get tired when I finally hit something. I can feel my elbow make contact. That's it though, no reaction to the pain. The disappointment sets in that this doesn't have the effect I desired. Then the left hand slips out from my grip.

We both go crashing into the pool. It's deep in there. I try to roll around which is a challenge due to my clothes. I can barely see but I do notice blending within the water is a dark red color. Takes me a second to realize I finally slipped out of his hold. The objective now is to get to the surface before he does or before he catches me.

I manage to get to the shallow part of the massive pool. I'm crawling out directly since I am exhausted from the struggle I went through and still being a bit drunk. I start to find it ironic I just came out of a pool of water and yet I'm dehydrated.

I go to touch the bridge of my nose. Some of the stitches came loose, blots of blood are on my finger.

"Aren't you tired of always limping away from our interactions?" I hear this being said behind me. His voice still invokes that spine chilling sensation.

I can't let him know that though. I turn my head, "aren't you tired of being a psychotic asshole?" I hear a light chuckle as a response.

I exhale and try to stand up as quickly as I can which isn't quick at all. I turn around to see him in nothing but his tighty whiteys. He's dripping wet with his blond hair pressed down. He still has that happy to see you smile on his face.

This time he's got blood gushing from his nose and a tooth missing. It gets into his mouth and stains the rest of his teeth. They become bright red like he just drank Pomegranate juice.

He spits out blood, "nice shot Champ," he states genuinely.

"Hey nice make up you have on, almost didn't see due to the blood gushing out of your nose. Oh wait, my mistake those are the bruises that I gave you when I was punching you in the face." I smirk as I wanted to give him a dig.

"How's the nose?" He gives it right back which dissolves my grin. While pointing a thumb towards the pool he then says, "I've been in there a while."

"How long is a while and how the hell did you know I'd be here?"

He chuckles, "you're so inquisitive, I find that refreshing. I can't also help but think that you feel like you really are a detective, you know, rather than just pretending to be one." He says as he smiles then spits.

"Would you stop spitting in the pool, if you haven't noticed we've been rolling around in here," I yell at him.

I am annoyed that he keeps doing that but it's also a way to ignore his comment, to show that it didn't affect me in the way he wanted it to. I try to add insult to injury. I change my tone and say, "for someone who smiles a lot you sure are an asshole."

He chuckles. Then he looks up with that smile and says, "It really is a beautiful day."

I also look up but with my arm out letting the big globs of rain water slap into the palm of my flat hand. "Are you for real?"

"Every day that I am alive and able to feel the weather on my face is the definition of a beautiful day." He says as he now has his head tilted back with his eyes closed.

"Aw jeez, are you like a religious nut or some shit?"

He puts his head back down to look at me. "Ha no, one can be enlightened by life without being spiritual. If anything what I believe in is planet Earth."

"I think I finally got the answer to the question what is worse than a religious nut, a goddamn hippie. Is that the reason why you stopped attacking me on the bus when those people came on?"

He changes his smile into a slight smirk. "No women, no children, all life is precious."

"Including the ones you kill for money?" I sharply ask.

His smirk transforms into a smile that shows all of his pearly whites as he puts his arms out. "What can I say, I'm a complicated man."

You know, I am glad we're finally having a real conversation rather than having you just stare at me with that dumb smile on your face like a retard." I say now trying to get a rise out of him.

No bite as he chuckles again. "I could hear your partner give out his war cry." He spits again despite my protest of doing so. This tug of war of attempting to piss the other off is heading to stalemate land. "He's not exactly quiet, is he?"

"He's not exactly my partner either," I say bluntly.

"Once we heard him I figured it was about to start. So I climbed out the window directly above the pool and jumped in. It's deep enough."

Something about that statement didn't sound right to me. I ask, "Those windows have no latches, they're not meant to be open. So how did you get out of them?" He answers by pointing up.

I squint to look up at where he came from and I see a frame where a plate glass window used to be. "You busted it open, I'm sure the fat man couldn't be too happy with you." Where he jumped from isn't directly over the pool he still could have broken his neck, too bad.

He keeps talking, "Then I waited in the pool. Not expecting you to come over here." I turn to look back at him. That's when I notice he's slowly moving his right hand down his leg.

I feel so dumb that I didn't spot the sheath that's attached to his right thigh. He's been trying to distract me this whole time with his conversational skills. Still, I'm usually more perceptive than that. To be honest I was too busy staring at his underwear, don't judge that's a weird sight.

I try to pretend that I don't see his hand get closer to his knife and casually look back up at the new side door he made. Hopefully he doesn't catch on due to being distracted with trying to kill me and the rain. "How did you not drown," I ask him.

"I was just going to sneak up behind you as you entered the house. But I got luckily." He says completely ignoring my question. He then grabs the handle of his giant hunting knife and starts to take it out. "Did I ever tell you why they call me Happy?"

His calling card before he kills someone. He's already told me that, what twice and nothing. I hope it pisses him off. While still looking up I dive into my pocket fumbling for my blade. I finally get it out, move my head to look back at him, and flip it out.

He's standing there with his knife out. Compared to his mine looks a foot smaller. I'm getting knife envy. Plus, I notice his has a hook at the end of it, the better to gut someone with.

As he gets into the 'I'm going to stomp on you now' stance I quickly think of something I can say. I have to be just as unpredictable as he is.

I open my mouth and say, "did anyone ever tell you why they call me Champ?"

"Yeah, it's a derivative from your last name." His response leaves me dumbfounded.

I let him see this though. I don't react and come up with the first thing that pops up. "Well yeah, but there's another reason why everyone calls me by my now famous moniker."

He gets curious as his brow frowns slightly and the big smile turns into a smirk but doesn't change his body language. Oh, and what's that," he asks unconvincingly.

Luckily my back is facing the side of the house that will lead to the front. I hadn't noticed we were circling each other like a Matador and a Bull. I just don't know which is which in this analogy.

"Well the thing is," I then turn around as fast as I can and bolt. To beat him I have to be just as ruthless and as unpredictable. Even if that means to tuck tail and run.

I hate running, especially in the rain. My left knee causes me to limp. Putting my knife back into my pocket I come across the hole that the second explosion caused.

This one is on the side right before the corner of the house. I try to quickly climb over the debris and go in. Moving becomes difficult due to my clothes sticking to my body from how wet they are.

I head inside to the grand staircase leading to the second floor of the mansion. The stairs pointed towards the heavens lead to hell as it is covered in bodies and you can hear the sounds of war. Most of them are Blood's army. What do you expect from mostly kids, but some of them are cops.

As I climb over the death I wonder if Wulf is up there. Maybe I can end this all tonight. Then I realize to do that the Happy situation that I am currently running away from has to be done with first.

I get to the top and immediately turn around looking for him but don't see anything. I take off my jacket. Keeping the contents inside except the blade, I take that. I head to the fat man's office which also happened's to be the source of the noise.

The two doors are off the hinges and on the floor. I walk through the naked doorway. I am presented with pandemonium.

Blood is on one side of the massive room fighting two guys at once. I have no intentions of getting rid of this guy. He is for now the lesser of two evils. I know that won't last long after the Mayor is gone. I am pretty sure he won't take this opportunity to whack me tonight either. I get the feeling he respects me, even likes me. Still that is no reason trust him.

On the other side is Rondo, the Mayor's bodyguard, also taking on two guys at once. It's like watching Frankenstein's monster attack the villagers. All Blood's guys need are torches and pitchforks. You know these two are going to eventually fight and it's going to be epic.

I look around the room glancing at all the little fights going on. I recognize some of the cops. Then I see him, Wulf.

His tall frame with his long arms has someone in a chokehold as he's punching him in the face while laughing. What a douche. This angers my blood so I take out my knife back out with the intention of slipping it into his back.

I start charging towards him blade in hand. Then in mid run I get tackled from the side. Its Happy, he brings me down sits on top of me, and says "excuse me."

"Get off you smiling jackass."

"I'm sorry but I can't do that." He says as he punches me in the face.

I move my head best I can so he doesn't break my nose open again. I can't stand going to the hospital. They think they know everything. My hands find their way around his throat. "I am going to choke that smile off your fucking face."

Ok here's the thing with this guy, he went from being mysterious to downright annoying. I'll admit he was scary and intimidating to me at first. I tried not to show that every time I saw him. He's unpredictable, smart, and fucking crazy. Let's not forget dangerous as well.

"You must know this is only a job. I feel like we're kindred spirits." He says in a distorted voice do to my choking him.

Blood said a similar thing. My response is "shut up." He responds back by punching my face again which is not going to make my nose look better.

I refuse to let go no matter how many times he hits me. Even if my nose gets broken or cut open again. Happy knows this, so he decides to place his hands together as if he were praying.

Their slipped under and then in between my arms. With one swoop he separates his hands and uses them like a wedge to separate my arms. He does this a few times until I lose my grip around his throat. It started to become difficult to stay in that position due to keeping my arms up for so long.

His whole thing was done pretty quickly but in my mind it went down a lot slowly. It dawns on me that was a Captain Thunder move number 43: How to break free from a frontal choke position.

I had dropped my blade when Happy tackled me to the ground. He switches roles and now wraps his hands around my throat. I can see the blade in the corner of my left eye lying next to me. I struggle to reach for it as his grip gets tighter. His smile once representing genuineness not just comes off really creepy in this position.

This must be done quickly. I manage to get a hold of the blade and I jam it into his left thigh. Nothing, no reaction, much to my surprise. I have no choice but to do it again. I take it out just to thrust it back into the same spot. His eyes never leave mine. Screw this, his lack of response isn't going to stop me from getting free.

My need for survival causes me to take my blade and repeatedly stab his thigh in multiple places at great speed. I would yell if he wasn't squeezing my windpipe. I'm still at a loss as he doesn't respond to one of many punctures I've made into his leg. The wounds are producing one massive pool of blood.

I don't have time to deduce why this isn't stopping him. I'm on the verge of blacking out and not the kind I'm usually looking forward to. I've wasted time on an idea that didn't work. My brain is scrambling on what to do and I don't have time left.

Then an idea dawns on me like a light shining on the ever growing darkness. I grab the blade and take it out of his leg. This becomes difficult at first since it was jammed in there pretty good, might have hit bone.

I place my blade under his chin. I'm having trouble keeping my arm up. Plus, as he's choking me my body moves so I'm trying not to execute my plan too early.

I speak having trouble getting my voice loud enough for him to hear me. "Hey, heyyyy." Neither my voice nor the sharp blade under his chin gets him to stop. I smack him in the face with my right as hard as the remaining energy I have allows me.

That gets him to notice. He snaps out of his trance to loosen his grip a bit. I move the pointy part of my blade to the side of his neck. "I will jam this under your jaw that you will literally taste the blood off the blade." I say barely.

He has a shocked look mixed with a small smile on his face when I was threatening him. Then it changed to a big smile as he says, "of course buddy!"

He gets off me. I stand up trying to clear my throat. We stand two feet from each other in the middle of chaos going on around us. Rondo and Blood are finishing their respective battle. The two biggest ones here will soon find each other bashing the others face in soon enough.

Wulf is finishing off a fight and the Mayor is nowhere to be seen. It's no surprise the one who started this is the one not here.

Still standing across from each other I don't see his huge knife. I feel like I have the advantage now. I know that's a false hope.

We go at it like two kids in the playground. Punching, kicking, pushing, and throwing each other around, it's a real brawl. Who am I kidding? He's faster than me and can fight better than me. Add to the fact I'm still out of it. Let's face it, he's beating the shit out of me.

It doesn't stop either of us from both huffing and puffing after a while. He has trouble standing due to his ever bleeding thigh. I'm having issues as well with my knee. All the stiches on my face have come off. Blood trickles down my face. His has gotten all over me as well.

"It must piss you off, been trying to kill me this whole time to no prevail." I say in a gravelly voice in between heavy breathing. I'm trying to bait him, he just smiles.

"Why did the Mayor want the Commissioner dead and that lead singer from that shitty band?" I ask as I need to know the answers to these old questions.

He shakes his head while laughing. "I really find you funny and silly. If only things were different between us. No matter what happens today, don't change. To answer your question, I kill people for money."

I have a confused look on my face. "What the hell are you talking about I know that." Then I finally understand, "they were just individual contracts?"

He smiles and nods his head, "that's right bud. The Commissioner wanted to kill himself but couldn't do it. He hires me, it looks like murder, and his family gets the life insurance."

"As for Johnny Dirtbag, turns out he had a lot of abandoned illegitimate children. The mother's got together, wanted him to pay for not paying. Then after he was dead they would fight what little estate he had after all the years of booze and drugs."

I am shocked. "I can't believe I was just in the wrong place at the wrong time."

"See, it's not always about you silly."

I would like the last word before we do this so I say, "you look ridiculous just standing in your underwear."

When I think I do he replies with, "it is what it is."

My blood starts to boil to the point where parts of my battered face that aren't already a different color start to turn red. I hate a many of things on this world, but I really despise that phrase.

Seriously, what the hell does that mean? 'I just got shot in the arm, it is what it is'. You have the god given right to bitch about a situation whether the outcome was created by you or not. If you get a flat tire while driving to your father's funeral by all means kick and curse at that tire while foaming at the mouth.

By standing there and just saying, 'it is what it is', it's almost as if you suppress that frustration deep down. Until it festers and you end up shooting people on top of a university tower. The people who use this phrase hide behind it. Rather than just saying, 'you know what, your right, this situation is fucked up.'

I don't communicate any of this to Happy. Instead I think I just grunt out some incoherent gibberish. I come up with a better follow up.

"I am going wipe that god damn smile off your face."

He responds with a smile, "You can try buddy."

Now at this point Happy is standing by the Mayor's desk. I come at him with full speed. My intention was to slam him up against the wall. Unfortunately, with the combination of everything going on plus with my adrenaline it doesn't pan out this way.

I didn't realize Happy was in front of the window overlooking the city.

There's a loud crash as we both go through the big plate glass window. Down we go but our drop is cut shorter than I expected. I get up drenched in water again.

It takes a second to realize we are on top of the grotto with the waterfall at our feet's. Happy starts to get up as I remember I never picked up my blade. He starts attacking me.

We start trading blows again but with less steam this time around. We are both bruised, bloody, and winded. With Happy looking much more pale and out of it than I am. This is probably due to his knife wounds. He stands there staggering but ever vigilant that he won't go down.

This is my moment to deliver the final blow. I know I being unpredictable is a must. I have to deliver such a debilitating blow that he won't be able to come back from it. That's when I kick his knee in.

Thrusting my foot diagonally downward towards his right knee. It pops backwards and causes him to go down with no facial expression.

As he's trying to hold himself up with one knee a gush of water pushes him over the edge. He falls back first and hits the pool. This is similar to when he hid in the water and surprised me. Except with a lot less blood.

I have to see this to the end. So I dive in the pool. I figure if he can do it twice, I'll be ok. Luckily I am. When I emerge from the water I notice most of it has blood in it. I feel like I'm swimming in Kool aid.

I find Happy or what's left of him, laying in the water. It's hard to see him because the water became so murky. I can definitely tell that he's dying.

Looking past the murkiness I see the piece of glass sticking out of his left side. This is due to crashing through the window. I hadn't noticed before his fall. It's making the blood flow out much faster. His face is still underwater. I kneel and pick up his head.

He's been holding his breath. He coughs up blood following with a smile. He doesn't say anything and neither do I. Its gets pretty uncomfortable with me kneeling on one knee holding up his head in the water. Good thing I don't have to feel my muscles get tense.

Eventually Happy starts to talk, "We are so much alike you and I."

That comment almost makes me want to drown him. "How the hell are you, a fucking psycho, anything like me?" Not that I'm such a prize.

He laughs then spits out more blood. "My father, not a very good man, once said to me that pain is for the weak. It stops a man from doing anything with his life. Pain turns into fear which turns you into a pussy. Pain and fear go hand and hand. Those two make you less of a man."

"You can't accomplish the kind of shit that life throws at you when you're afraid of being in pain. The real men are the ones who look at pain and without so much as a fart keep going."

This sounds like a lovely guy, my father and his should get together and discuss the problems with minorities. He goes on, "They can say they weren't turned into slaves by pain. When the time comes that homo Death will come."

"You will look deep into his empty eye sockets. Then can you say to his bony face that you lived a life without pain or fear? If you can, well then boy you will have died a man and a winner. Be a winner boy, don't be a loser."

"You have a gift the weak would kill for. It's an easy win for your boy, your already half way to being a true man. All you have to do is grow up and stop fucking whining. Then he would hit me."

His words roll around in my head. I quickly try to analyze them. That is pretty damn close to what Blood said to me then what I repeated to Powers but this version emphasis more on pain. It gets me thinking about things that happen and what people have said.

'You two warriors are intertwined, equally strong, equally dangerous'. 'We are so much alike you and I', plus the fact he didn't react to his knee or the multiple stab wounds I gave him. Then like someone who hasn't gotten a joke told twenty years ago it dawns on me.

"You have **congenital analgesia**?" I ask him slowly with my brow scrunched due to confusion.

"Now you finally get it." He says as I want to slap my forehead because

I feel so dumb right now. "We're two sides to a coin. The Mayor hired me to hunt you down and kill you. But when I found out you had what I had, I wanted to learn more about you. Then I tried to kill you."

"I have no ill will towards you. We're like brothers. In a different time and place, who knowns. Also I won't really die, I'll live on, through you."

I look into his eyes for the first time realizing their green, like mine. I think about all the things he did or tried to do to me. He broke my nose, he tried to kill me a few times, and my face is swollen and bloody because of him. Maybe it's a mixture of the events leading up to this moment. Or the fact that this scene feels so tripe and cliché.

Either way it wants me to do something drastic. As I hold his dying head I respond to him and say, "No you won't," then I drop his head in the water and walk away.

For the first time since I met this homicidal maniac that his perpetual smile has slowly turned into a frown.

I limp my way back upstairs to the office. On the way there before the giant stairwell is one of Blood's men stuck to the wall by Happy's hunting knife. Now I know why he didn't have it on him.

Seeing the knife helps me dawn on something. "Damn, I forgot to ask him why he killed that bartender. Oh well, no point going back."

Entering the office almost everyone is dead or knocked out. I curse myself as I don't see Wulf around. He must have ran off knowing his moments were numbered. No honor amongst thieves and all.

I didn't miss the main event however as Blood and Rondo are fighting. It's like watching King Kong versus Godzilla. Blows are being traded. Whatever is left intact in this office is now being thrashed by them throwing each other around.

These combatants seem equally matched but only in size. Rondo is actually taller but his wide frame is more due to 'fat muscle', kind of like Andre the Giant. Whereas Blood is wide due to muscle, pure muscle.

The dope looks like he bench presses a clown car filled with his brainwashed servants. I've had a lot of head trauma so that's the best analogy I can come up with.

Every punch and every slap comes with its own thunderclap. For a second I find myself taken out of the fight of the, week I guess, to notice that I don't see the Mayor. In fact, I do not remember seeing him this whole time.

Back to the fight it looks like Rondo is getting tired. Although he looks strong he lacks the stamina that Blood seems to exceed in part to lifting clown cars.

A final blow landed across Rondo's face causes him to collapse. Blood picks up the giant and slams him onto the Mayor's oak desk breaking it into two. The expensive looking piece of furniture became the only item in the office that hadn't been destroyed.

Blood is huffing and puffing standing over the body with his face paint mostly off. I walk over to him and say, "Good job," as I flash a thumbs up and a wink in his direction. I then look around the room and I state the obvious, "where's the Mayor?"

His chest is still heaving in and out. The beads of sweat are running down his bald head bringing the face paint with it as it rolls down.

He points behind me at a lavish oak book shelve. Most of the shelves have been knocked down. The rest of Blood's men which consists of a small number, have axes and are chopping away at the rest of the shelves.

"The Mayor thinks he can hide behind his technology. He will come to realize, he is mistaken," says the new Intercontinental Champion. "The fat pig is behind a wall of steel and wires, but we will get to him."

"So he's in a panic room? Why the hell can't you just say that?" Blood then is given a gun by one of his followers. He swivels around and the gun is pointed in my direction. My hands come half way up, "Whoa, whoa, just kidding."

Then I take a second to think. I put my hands down. Then I say, "You know what, fuck it, do it, then I don't have to hear your riddles and testosterone fueled monologues anymore."

He raises the gun past my head and shoots behind me at the ceiling. He hits a camera that was positioned in the corner. Must be hooked up to the room. The brainwashed chop up the rest of the wooden shelves. What's revealed behind it is a large metal door with a keypad.

"Now is the time of our reckoning! We will tear in like a tin can!" He yells all of this.

"How the hell are you going to do that, with axes? That shit's probably a few inches thick." I say as I try hard to refrain from saying that's what she said.

"No, with this." A drone walks up behind him with putty in his hands. Then they walk up to the metal door.

"Is that C4," I ask shockingly.

"That is right, I told you Hill can get just about anything."

"No, you didn't say that exactly." The drone places wires inside the C4, "and are we going to get out of here before this thing blows?"

Everyone starts to leave except for Blood. There's a timer in the putty. I walk out fast, because frankly I don't run, even for a fucking bomb.

Everyone goes into the hallway. I grab my jacket from the floor and head for the bottom of the stairs. I move my head slightly and cover my ears so not to get into the same situation as last time. I am now staring into the dead eyes of Happy's victim still stuck to the wall.

A giant boom follows causing me to squint. I walk up the stairs and the ones left alive are on the floor withering in pain. Inside the room everything is demolished.

Parts of the ceiling and the walls have come off exposing the cement. The windows have all but shattered.

Standing in the doorway is Blood with nothing but tethered clothes.

Any of the bodies that were laying around are nothing but stains. That includes Rondo, who may not have been dead, but now looks like a Jackson Pollack painting.

The only thing that stands is the metal door. You can almost hear the fat man laughing behind it. The big man looks pissed but doesn't show it.

As I move closer to him I see he does have some scratches on his chest, doubt he even feels them. Some of his men get up and in a dazed stupor start to run off, down the stairs and into the night.

Blood puts his hand behind his back and just stares at the metal door. He says to me without turning his head, "has Senior Feliz been takin care of?"

I scoff at his dramatic expressions. "Yeah, he's been put on ice." I walk over to the shattered window. "Well no not ice, let me do that again, he's been cooled off." I start to stick my head out, careful of any loose pieces of glass, to gloat in my glory.

"Jeez, that attempt at a one-liner was even wors- damn it!" Happy's body is missing. I stick my head in yelling, "oh all the clichéd, who the hell does he think he is, Michael Myers?"

Blood lets out a loud bellowing laugh. "Why the hell are you laughing? You can't get the goddamn door open." Then I change the expression on my face because something dawns on me. "You knew his body would be gone."

"Yes, I knew, because he is la cucaracha who does not die."

"Well tell me, Mr. Montoya, how did you know he had the same medical condition that I do?"

"A master does not reveal his secrets."

"You had him followed didn't you?"

He lowers his head and says, "Yes."

One of the guys who ran off came back disproving my theory that that fucker just ran home. He hands Blood something making sure not to reveal it.

Blood blows the secret by spinning around and holding it high between his thumb and first finger. It is a small grenade but it looks different, it's blue and black, like something out of Star Trek.

"It is an EMP grenade." He says proud and before I can even ask.

"An EMP," I still ask with a confused and surprised look on my face.

"Yes," he responds while smiling at the future bomb. "An Electromagnetic Pulse-"

"I know what it is." I cut him off and am offended this painted up crack head would assume I wouldn't know what that was.

"Essentially it will shut down all the electronics and turn that massive vault door into a screen door, easily accessible. How do you know there isn't some defense set up in the panic room for this sort of thing? Plus, won't this thing create a blackout throughout the city, you don't need that kind of heat right now."

"On the contrary my negative friend, this particular device can only produce a pulse strong enough for this house. It will probably reach our cars. Which will not be effected for they are turned off. And as for the security of the door, I will wait until the earth opens to swallow us all."

"Why the hell would that happen?" My question falls on deaf ears. I should really just go but I need to see this guy dead more so than Blood does. Why is it taking so long? I thought I would get rid of Happy, which I fucking didn't, and this Mayor boil would be lopped off my ass. The real lopping off procedure would be quicker.

Blood twists the top and bottom of the EMP in different directions. It starts to glow green. He calmly places it in front of the door. I shake my head and go back to my spot at the bottom of the stairs. This time I don't stare at the dead eyes hung on the wall. I impatiently anticipate this shit going off as I grab my flask and take a drink.

Another explosion, but this one doesn't cause me to cover my ears. The noise can best be described as an old dial up modem trying to connect to the internet. Add more of a screeching effect to it.

The room fills up with a bright blue light show that spools over into the hallways illuminating onto the ceiling. It becomes so bright that they seem to phase through the walls.

It's a laser light show and no one brought the Pink Floyd music or the munchies. Have to be honest though, it's pretty despite its destruction purposes.

A few seconds later it ends. I head up and once again Blood is just standing in the doorway smiling like a crazy person.

I look out the whole in the wall that used to be a window overlooking the city. I can see the rest of Kalani which is shrouded in darkness. I say to him, "uh, chuckles, your little matrix bomb took out the whole neighborhood."

His expression changes from smiles to dismissive as he waves his hand and he says, "No matter."

I shake my head and mutter to myself, "low profile."

One of the disciples comes with a crowbar, another one a battery operated lamp that illuminates the room. Three of them trying to pry the door open at once. As funny as this is I am very impatient as I want this ridiculous shit to end.

Blood stands their arms crossed his smile transforms into a frown. His face becomes menacing and red.

Then as his anger boils to rage he screams, "Enough." He pushes all three men away, grabs the crowbar all the while screaming. "Life tried to best me, that puta tried to best me, even the fat man in his cage has tried. They have all failed."

Every grunting moment between strenuously pulling the crowbar to pry the door is filled with words. "I. Will. Not. Be bested. By this. Maldito door."

So first he was channeling Khan, now it's an impression of Kirk he's doing. With that final push this metal door that prevented me from finishing this annoying chapter in my life comes ripping open.

Inside are concrete walls with no windows. There's a cot and a wall covered in multiple monitors with a dashboard in front. On the screens are displayed with different areas like the side of the house with the hole in it, the bloody grotto pool, and the one that was in the office which is just static now.

The Mayor is cowering in the corner that faces the cot. I notice he's just bending down and not on the floor. I make a mental note that he must have been too fat to kneel or crouch so bending his back down was the best thing he could do.

He holds on to something to push himself upright. The whimpering starts immediately. "Please don't do dis." His accent that he tried to pull off as intimidating which became more of a caricature is still there but has become sadder. His glasses are off and tears are streaming down his face.

Blood doesn't say anything as he grabs him by the back of his neck and pushes him out into the room formerly known as his office.

His whining gets louder when he sees the condition of the room. "My office! It was so lavish. Youse destroyed my paintings." Blood forces him to kneel in the middle of the room facing the view to the city. His face expresses pain due to the kneeling.

Just then he recognizes a piece of human flesh that used to be Rondo. I don't know how he knew but it's fittingly lying on the pile of tinder that was once his decadent desk.

"Rondo, my sweet, sweet Rondo. Youse butchered my son youse animals." He attempts to spit on the same man that he was just pleading to seconds ago but fails as nothing comes out.

Blood takes a step away from him as he turns his head to look at me and nods. It's my sign to say or do what I have to before he's dealt with. I walk over to the cracked Humpty Dumpty with the curiosity in my head before anything. "You mean to tell me that freak show was your kid?"

He turns to notice me. "Champ, Champ, save me, I'll do anythings, I'll give youse money," he says hysterically and frantically.

I half turn to see Blood in the corner of my eye and say while smirking, "I have a feeling getting your money is not going to be an issue."

The blubbering mess keeps going as I get closer to him. "Youse'll save me, won't youse? Youse won't let dese animals murder me. Youse the hero."

I start to get mad. "There is no hero to this story. You made damn sure of that. Whatever fucked up personality I turned into you helped create."

"You said it yourself, to never forget you had a hand in this. So here I am. You may have indirectly murdered my friend and his family but I am tired of having you directly murder the English language."

Blood's shadow looms over me as he comes up and puts his hand on my shoulder. "Do what you will my brother, judge him as the lord will, share with him the pain he has given you."

My right hand becomes a fist as it starts shaking. A spark inside my mind tells me 'this isn't right'. I try to ignore it. My conscience gets louder. I am a trapeze artist forever balancing on the wire of my morality. I want to hit him and I do not care about the moral consequences of that act.

Then my self-righteousness chimes in. 'Don't be like them,' it says. It dawns on me that I may not care about the effect beating the crap out of this horrible person may have on me. However, I do care if the meathead behind me thinks that we're on the same level that he can call me a 'brother'.

I am better than him and not because I am a good person or a hero. It's just due to the fact that I just am better than Brother Blood. I just am better than the Mayor. So much so that I will not deal with this situation violently. In fact, I will deal with this in the best way I know how, like a vindictive smart ass.

I release my fist, remove Blood's hand from my shoulder and lean into the Mayor's face. "I am not going to hit you. Instead take my words to your grave with what little life you have left. There are repercussions in the decisions we make in life."

"Your dream is dead. You're so called empire, dead."

"When these guys are finished taking everything that's not bolted down the scavengers will come out of the woodwork to pick off whatever's left. Your operation will be pulled apart by whichever generals are still alive."

"Speaking of which, all the drugs are now Blood's. Additionally, that dream of yours to own a movie studio is up in smoke. The final piece, the final insult."

I put my hand in my pocket and pull out the little confessional tape. I recognize I am very lucky for still having despite all the tumbling around I did.

"I am going to send this to every newspaper. Everything you built and wanted is gone. The worse part, your name which is all that you have left will be dragged into the mud. You will always be remembered as nothing more than a lowlife criminal."

"These are the repercussions for the fucked up decisions you made in life."

When I'm done speaking he puts his head down, starts to sob, and tears drop down on the floor. I turn around to face Blood. He looks disappointed but says "every problem has its own solution, eh mi amigo?"

I look up at him to say, "I am not your friend," then I walk away.

Blood steps closer to the crying Mayor, "the last moments of your life starts now."

The Mayor's beating went on for a while. Blood turns around huffing and puffing with his hands red and covered in the Mayor's blood. They look like they've been punching a side of freshly cut beef. It's hard for me to look at the fat turd as he's wincing. His breathing has a wheeze to it.

It's called a death rattle. Your whole life ending in a few moments represented as a creepy sound. It makes you sound sad and useless. I couldn't give a shit whether the Mayor makes it but it gives my PTSD a jolt. I start to flashback as all I see is Charlie lying on the floor with the same shallow breathing.

I have to look away as this scene hits too close to home. Blood cracks his knuckles and says, "We finish this."

He takes his final step to the future dead man who can only make a faint whimper. I turn my head back to see rage on Blood's face as he pushes his thumbs deep into the Mayor's eye sockets. His wheezing becomes a blooding curdling moan.

This torturing is torture for me, I take a swig from the flask to try numb my brain. It's not the content of the act but instead how long it's taking. Also the noise he's producing is disturbing to me due to the PSTD.

Finally, the moans along with his era fade into nothing. Then Blood stops turns to me with his upper body mostly covered in blood and says, "The king is dead."

Whereas I then mutter to myself, "long live the king."

Blood then says to me, "it is done, you have nothing to fear anymore. Are you ready to leave my friend?"

I give him a what-are-you-talking-about-Willis kind of look. "This wasn't about fear."

Then it dawns on me, "I don't know what this was about. This started off about me, it always does. Maybe not revenge but a way to unleash some aggression I still had. Who better than the man indirectly responsible? Then it evolved into preventing that sack of shit from doing this to anyone else.

It was still about me. Now it was really about Astra. It was about all the families and businesses he stepped on to keep this city under his thumb."

I look pass Blood and see the dead bloated body that started this long chain of dominos.

"I really thought, maybe a part of me would be closer to peace. I also thought I'd be dead at the end of the night. I guess both thoughts were wrong. There's still going to be that day that I say the wrong thing and instead of a beating I'll end up dead. Just thinking about that sweet relief gets me gitty."

I turn from looking at the lifeless bloated tick and look down at the floor. I go into the blackouts. I can't help but think all these jokers I've encounter on this strange journey can be argued as a twisted version of me somehow.

Powers is the road I could have went down if I had become a corrupt cop. The Mayor is a persona I might have turned into if that corruption kept going and became absolute.

Blood represents my guilt which could have turned me mad instead of an asshole.

Then there's Happy. He was the first potential change I could have made. If I had grown up differently. If my birth defect took me down the path it took him, I could have been the smiling homicidal jackass.

I snap out of my trance and look out of what used to be windows at the bright lights of the cesspool I sort of call home. I take a swig as I notice it looks much brighter with a gated community of darkness in front of it. It also looks like, false hope.

"This city swallowed me whole, when it spit me out I became mutilated. I know it's not close to being over because there will be many who will try to take the throne that we just made empty."

I do my best Batman impression, "that means Wulf is still out there." Then I remember something and I say normally, "oh yeah and Happy."

I can hear being said behind me in a Ricardo Montalban accent, "Brother Blood was just looking for you to say you needed a ride." I shake my head and take a swig.

Made in the USA
Middletown, DE
28 August 2016